Gumshoe Granny Investigates

A Bess Bullock Retirement Home Mystery

by

Allen B. Boyer

For information, email **Cozy Cat Press**, cozycatpress@aol.com or visit our website at: www.cozycatpress.com

COZY CAT
P R E S S

ISBN: 978-0-9848402-0-5
Printed in the United States of America

Cover design by Cecilia Rockwell
http://coversbycecilia.daportfolio.com/

10 9 8 7 6 5 4 3 2 1

DEDICATION

For Mae Gruber, who could charm the socks off the world.

For Ruth Moore, who always wanted to learn more about
the world.

IMPOSTER IN THE GARDEN

He was clearly not the gardener. While he dressed in the proper uniform, carried the correct tools, and appeared every so many days to check on the plants at her retirement home, she knew he was not the gardener.

It was a very subtle thing to notice. Bess Bullock made her observations known to one of the nurses who worked at the Honey Hills Retirement Home. However, the nurse, like so many other nurses at Honey Hills, was too busy dispensing medicine and delivering food to look out the window when Bess presented them with her question. She could recall how one nurse barely glanced at the man's clothes before deeming him a gardener and Bess's suspicions of him merely confusion. Bess learned early on that confusion was the reason given by nurses to any resident whose thoughts or actions wavered from the norm. It was for this reason alone that Bess usually kept such suspicions and observations to herself. However, in this particular case, Bess knew that her suspicions about the gardener were correct.

Unlike the nurses who spent their day making rounds and dispensing medicine, Bess Bullock had an abundance of time on her hands. An abundance of time that came with retirement. Lately, Bess was using this abundance of time to sit by the window of her small room, look out, and study what this man did, or more importantly, did not do to the flowers, weeds, and other things growing in the courtyard garden.

First, there was the random nature with which he chose to pull weeds. Any gardener worth his weight knows that a thorough weeding job in a garden requires one to pull from end to end. A full pile of weeds is usually the result from a satisfactory day of weeding. This so-called gardener was simply looking around and pulling one or two weeds every time he came, choosing to ignore many others.

Another clue Bess picked up on was how he tended to ignore some of the brightly colored flowers that were in need of water. It had been a dry summer, maybe one day of light rain every other week. She knew that the plants in the garden needed to be watered every other day to keep them thriving. The gardener in question was very limiting in his use of water. He tended to focus on one particular plant in the garden— a small green leafy plant— while choosing to ignore the flowers that were struggling to grow. Bess went outside one day after the man left and touched the ground around the flowers.

"Dry as a walnut," she remembered mumbling to herself.

As the weeks went by, she began to see him spending more time around that one particular plant in the garden. The small green plant looked like a weed, Bess thought, and didn't appear to hold any special significance. After a few weeks, and a few visits to the garden, Bess began to recognize the plant, and with it, the intent of the man claiming to be a gardener.

Being a former police officer proved to be her greatest advantage, and the greatest disadvantage for the young man she had been observing.

This morning, when she sat by the window and saw him appear, Bess quickly picked up the phone and dialed a number.

"He's here," she spoke into the phone. "Yes, I'm quite certain it's a marijuana plant. Yes, my name is Bess Bullock. I spoke with someone last week about this matter.

Yes, I saw him plant it myself. I am calling from the Honey Hills Retirement Home. You sent an officer here just a few days ago to examine the plant. Better hurry if you want to catch him."

She put the phone down and gazed out the window, watching the so-called gardener do his usual random pulling of weeds and his minimal watering of the plants. Her observations from her window were suddenly interrupted by a knock at the door.

"Come in," Bess said, her eyes glancing away from the window.

The door slowly opened, revealing her daughter, Samantha. Bess smiled then glanced over to a framed picture on top of the television of a young girl with chubby cheeks, long dark hair and a full bright smile. Bess looked back at the older version of her daughter standing before her and could feel her smile fade.

A divorcing mother of one, Samantha's cheeks were more flushed and less chubby. Her smile was less bright and more of an interruption between hectic moments. Her presence was that of a knowing adult, not the preschooler lacking in confidence that Bess had once known many years ago. No, Bess thought, if anything, Samantha no longer lacked in confidence.

"Samantha, my dear," Bess said with a slight grin. She reached up and grabbed her daughter's hand. "I thought it would be you."

"I told you I was coming," Samantha sighed, pulling up her cell phone and glancing at it with the kind of scowl one might use after discovering some type of bug crawling on their person. "I thought you'd be ready, Mom. We need to go to the bank. You remember the papers we have to sign? I'm only on lunch break for a short time so we really need to get going."

"I know," Bess replied, glancing out the window at the gardener. "We've had this discussion before, Samantha. I told you I'm not signing any papers."

"We've been through this, Mom," Samantha snapped, jabbing her cell phone in the air like a sword. "You're not going to spend the money you have in the bank. Now that you're here, you get all of your meals, a room, people to wait on you and help you. There's no reason for you to have money anymore. You're retired, mother. All you have to do is sit back and…enjoy it."

"Just because I'm in a retirement home doesn't mean I don't have dreams," Bess explained, her eyes narrowing at her daughter in a look that only a mother could convey. "I may wish to travel some day. It costs money to do something like that, you know."

"Some day?" Samantha laughed, "Mom … you're going to be eighty. You need to start thinking about how to be retired and not worry about doing things so much."

"My mother lived to be a hundred, as did my father," Bess quickly pointed out. "I may be turning eighty, but I'm still counting on another twenty years, Samantha. Don't talk to me about retirement like it's some…privilege. Now you wanted me to move into this place so I wouldn't be a burden to you. I quietly agreed to it. You should be happy with that."

"Mom, that's not why…I just wanted you to have some security," Samantha interrupted with a guilty tone. "I mean…what if you fell? Now that you're here…a nurse can help you if you fall."

"That's very nice, dear," Bess sighed. Her words were met with silence. "Like I said, Samantha, there won't be any papers signed today. I may be in a retirement home…but I'm still trying to figure out what that means for me. I know what it doesn't mean…giving away all my money. I just know I still have purpose."

With those final words, Bess forced her eyes away from Samantha and back out the window. There she saw a policeman talking to the alleged gardener. Bess could feel her back straighten as she saw the officer point at the small green plant that Bess had suspected was marijuana. The same plant the man had so diligently watered all these weeks. After a few seconds, she saw the policeman grab the man by the arm and lead him away. The conflict had ended as quietly as it had begun, Bess thought.

After she watched the officer escort the young man from sight, Bess turned to see that her daughter was no longer in the room. All that remained was the door slowly closing. Bess sat back for a moment, reflecting on her conversation with her daughter. Like the conflict outside of her window, the one in her room had also ended with an uncomfortable silence.

BRIDGE FOR FIVE

"It's not a bad life."

They were the words that Bess Bullock spoke to herself every once in a while. When she first moved into the Honey Hills Retirement Home seven months ago, Bess found her new surroundings a bit challenging. There were numerous hallways to negotiate, all of which looked the same to her. The similarity of the hallways presented her with some challenges in finding the correct room to attend a program or meeting.

Another challenge came in getting to know some of the people who lived at Honey Hills. Because she was new, Bess found people going out of their way to talk to her. Bess endured numerous conversations that helped her to learn some names, ages, and life stories of the Honey Hills's residents. She also got to learn about numerous ailments that were freely offered up in the conversations. The fact that she had no ailments to share in return seemed to always bring most conversations to a swift and unexpected close.

One thing she had to get used to was accountability. She was not accustomed to going to a nurse's station and signing her name in a book whenever she left the building to take a walk or take the bus to the store for a card or a newspaper.

"I'm a grown woman," Bess grumbled to one young nurse perched over the sign-out book. "I should be able to come and go without signing my name in that book."

Accountability was not the only adjustment for Bess. There was also the matter of her privacy. Throughout the day more than one nurse would randomly walk in and out of her room. Some were kind enough to knock before entering. Other nurses were less respectful, flinging open her door without warning. During their many visits, the nurses would bring Bess everything from medication, to a drink, to even an occasional snack. While they visited, the nurses would also slip in familiar questions to gauge how Bess was feeling.

"I'm fine!" was the standard response Bess would give.

Having lived at the Honey Hills Retirement Home for nearly seven months, Bess was now familiar with most of the residents and most of the details of her new life. She knew what programs took place on what days. She knew what meals she liked and what she didn't like in the dining hall. She had even committed to memory every detail of every hallway to the point where she knew where to go to find the best views outside at different times throughout the day.

Since Honey Hills was located near two farms in the Pennsylvania Dutch Country, Bess discovered numerous windows where she could enjoy views of farm land and fields. Some days Bess would walk to the south wing of the center where she could sit and watch cows graze in a field. There were other days when she walked to the north wing of the center to sit by a window and watch cars come and go from the Honey Hills' parking lot. She even knew of a window in the east wing where she could see the occasional tractor drive by.

Unlike the small town of Venton, where Bess raised her family, she liked living in the country. She liked stepping outside and not hearing the recurring sounds of passing trucks or cars. She liked the smell of fresh air without the hint of smog. She liked being able to hear birds chirp and notice the many ways that the wind could stir leaves on a tree.

It seemed to Bess that all retirement homes should always be located in such a quiet place. After living for many years, Bess thought, retirement should mean having a quiet place to walk, think and reflect on one's life. While she wasn't happy about giving up her house and moving to a retirement home, Bess was grateful that her daughter was able to find a place like the Honey Hills Retirement Home.

Despite her unsettled feelings about moving, there was plenty to like. When she walked along the blue rug that lined the hallways, there was always pleasant music playing over the speakers. When she'd pass by a room, she'd see someone watching a Bing Crosby movie or a Gene Kelly movie on television. Sometimes, Bess would stop to comment on her fondness for both performers.

During her meals, when she spoke to the ladies at her table about musicians like Mitch Miller or Tommy Dorsey, there was an instant recognition on the part of the resident with whom she was talking. There also seemed to be a general admiration for both musicians among the people she sat with for breakfast, lunch, and dinner, which Bess liked.

Everyone at the Honey Hills was nice, which after working for years as the first and only woman on her town's police force, was a welcome change of pace for Bess. Still, even though she was in a "retirement" home, she was finding it difficult to accept retirement. This was especially true for her instincts as a police officer.

Whenever she saw a face in the hallway, it took some adjusting for Bess to look at the face and *not* try to read it. *Not* try to look beneath the surface of the face to figure out what kinds of thoughts and feelings were lingering. While it served her well as a police officer, Bess now found her instincts to be distracting. Perhaps, she reasoned, her instinct to read others would eventually fade away. After all, she was surrounded by retirees. Once she got used to living in a place with people who were not motivated by greed, or lust, or anger, her skills for observing their actions and thinking about their behavior would be used less and less. Like any thing that is no longer used, Bess expected her investigative skills to grow useless and simply wither away. She knew it would take some time to happen. Yet, she looked forward to the day when she could be just a normal person, taking others at face value and not looking for their hidden motives or agendas. A day when she truly felt like she was truly retired.

On Tuesdays, Bess was part of a Bridge Club that would get together and share conversation as well as tips on sound strategies at winning a hand of bridge. This morning, the discussion was about the news that a drug dealer had been arrested on the grounds of the Honey Hills Retirement Home. As she looked around the table, Bess was well acquainted with the other three ladies in attendance.

Flo Morgenstern was the best dealer at the table. Bess was always mesmerized by how quickly Flo's fingers could dance around a deck of cards when she shuffled them. Her fingers moved with the precision of ten little sticks rubbing together to start a fire from the playing cards. Flo had spoken to Bess more than once about her years of working at the casinos as a Blackjack dealer. Her career began in Las Vegas before she retired to Atlantic City. Flo's husband was also employed as a Blackjack dealer. They retired in New Jersey for many years until Flo was widowed, and eventually moved to Pennsylvania and the Honey Hills Retirement Home.

Rose Grumbine ran a chain of flower shops that she got from her parents, who were also florists. Rose, an only child, often joked that having parents in the flower business left them with few choices for her name. Rose had a sensitive nose, perhaps because of her line of work. On more than one occasion, she would announce during a card game what she thought she smelled being prepared for supper, even though the kitchen was a few hallways away.

The third person at the table was Helen Gruber. Helen was married to a farmer and her farm was located just down the street from Honey Hills. When Helen's husband died, she reluctantly chose to sell the farm to developers because her children had no interest in continuing the farming tradition. As a result of her decision to sell, Helen was known as one of the richest women at Honey Hills. Some rumors had her at well over a million dollars from all the land she'd sold. Still, Helen quietly went about her life wearing the same dresses, having the same sense of humor about things, and genuinely enjoying the company of her friends on Tuesday mornings.

"Why on earth would a drug dealer come here?" Flo Morgenstern asked while shuffling cards. She peaked over her glasses with her sparkling blue eyes, and her pink lips melted into a smile. "If those police are really out to get someone, they should walk down to the pharmacy and arrest those scoundrels for what they're charging me for my blood pressure medicine!"

"It's a dangerous world out there," Helen Gruber mumbled. Helen tended to play with what little hair she had left when they were at the card table. It didn't matter what card game they played, Helen would twirl her few strands of hair with her fingers. A cancer survivor, no one ever mentioned her hair to Helen and she never discussed it. "Why just the other day I was out for a walk and a car came whizzing around the corner. Nearly knocked me clean off the road! The speed limit is clearly marked at fifteen miles per hour. That car must have been doing at least twenty."

"I agree with you, Helen," Bess nodded. "It is a dangerous world out there. Why, when I was a police officer in my hometown of Venton, things were different. Venton was a small town and I was the first woman on the force. I had a few blocks in town to walk every day. Over the years I got to know the people who lived and worked along those blocks. The worst thing that could happen back then would be the occasional argument between neighbors. I always felt it was my job to help them settle their arguments in a way that left both parties happy. Sometimes there would be the occasional theft of a piece of fruit from the grocery store, but that was about as bad as things got."

"You told us this before," Flo mumbled. She paused and looked at Bess. "How long did you say you worked for the police?"

"I was a police officer until I had Samantha," Bess replied. "In my ten years with the police I never had to draw my gun once. My words and my mind were all I needed to resolve problems back then. My daughter drove me through Venton the other week. When I looked at the streets of Venton today, well, I'm afraid I'd need more than words to do my job."

"I still can't believe you worked for the police," Flo mumbled, her eyes peering over her glasses at Bess. "Look at you! You're just such a little thing."

Rose Grumbine cleared her throat. Rose never said too much at the table. She came to play cards and throw out an occasional observation. She was not much of a talker, yet Bess found that she had keen observations to make about the people who lived at Honey Hills. When she spoke, Bess tended to give her words a bit more attention.

"On a different note," Rose quietly stated while staring at her cards. "Alma Crisp isn't doing well."

"How so?" Bess quickly asked, lowering her cards.

"I don't know," Rose explained, her eyes turning to Bess. "She sits at my table for meals and in the last couple of weeks she's been quiet, moody, saying things that she normally wouldn't say."

"Maybe she's pregnant," Helen laughed. "That's how I was when I was expecting. I was moody and speaking my mind."

Bess looked around and could see how the other ladies at the table simply smiled at the comment while they continued on with the game.

"Have you spoken with her?" Bess asked. "Have you asked how she's feeling?"

"I've tried," Rose sighed. She lowered her cards and shook her head. "There's just something about the tone in her voice. Her choice of words. Her appearance. Oh, where to begin. Have you noticed her appearance? Alma is usually impeccably dressed and easy to smile at a story or a joke. Lately, her hair is in all directions. Her clothes are wrinkled. I believe she is sleeping in her clothes. She just doesn't look well."

"Perhaps she got some bad news," Bess observed. She looked around the table. "Maybe she's just feeling blue. We all tend to feel that way from time to time. Old age and this place can wear any of us down. We all know that. That's one reason why we formed our little group, so each of us can help the other person when they feel down. Perhaps we should invite Alma to join our group?"

"Can't play bridge with five people," Flo snapped, staring at the cards in her hand. "A fifth player at a bridge table is like…a fifth wheel."

"I would be more than happy to take turns with her," Bess quietly answered. "I like Alma. I think we should help her if we can."

"Fine," Flo replied. "Then are we all okay with this decision?"

The rest of the table nodded or smiled in an unspoken but unanimous vote of agreement to ask Alma Crisp to join them every Tuesday morning for a game of bridge.

"Good," Bess nodded. "I actually go by her room on the way to my room. I'll stop and ask her to join us next Tuesday. I'm sure she will be most appreciative."

A few hours later, Bess was shuffling back to her room after a good morning of conversation and cards. She walked with a smile on her face. She usually smiled because of the time spent talking and laughing with her friends. If there was one thing that was desperately needed at Honey Hills, Bess thought, it was the sound of laughter to replace the silence.

Wherever she went in the Honey Hills Retirement Home, there tended to be silence accompanying her. Silence in the rooms. Silence in the halls. Silence in the dining room. Every once in a while Bess longed for a loud argument. A rambunctious party. Even a chorus of hearty laughter. There seemed to be an unspoken mission among the nurses to maintain an atmosphere of silence for its residents. While Bess understood that the silence was part of the service she was paying for, it didn't make her like it anymore.

When Bess stepped into her hallway, her eyes lingered on the blue rug that stretched out before her. Daylight sprayed through the windows, casting bright squares of light on the floor. Bess turned her eyes out the window and reminded herself of the weatherman forecasting a hot and humid summer day. Such a day was best viewed, Bess thought, from a large window in an air conditioned room. Her eyes squinted at the sunlight, the bright blue sky, and the green grass that was looking tall and uneven. Bess spent her share of summers cutting the grass at her home after her husband died. She quite liked not having to worry about such jobs when the days were bright and hot.

Bess reached the end of the hallway, turned a corner and stopped at the door to the room of Alma Crisp. Bess raised her hand to knock, then stopped to think about what she would say and what she would see. Would Alma smile when she walked in? Would she simply stare out the window and not acknowledge Bess? The bottom line was that she didn't know what to expect. With that uncertain expectation in mind, Bess simply grabbed hold of the door handle and pushed open the door.

The first thing that came into view was an empty chair by the window. Bess turned her eyes to the other side of the room where Alma's bed was located. Blocking her view of the bed was a woman. Bess could see the back of the woman's head with long dark hair going over her shoulders. Bess looked down at the sneakers and blue jeans the woman was wearing and quickly deduced that this was not a nurse.

"Alma?" Bess whispered to herself.

She took a step into the room and moved in the direction of the woman. When she looked at the bed, Bess saw what appeared to be two feet lying under the sheet. Another step and she could see an arm lying on top of the sheet. Another step and she could see a body that Bess thought belonged to Alma. However, the woman in the jeans was leaning too far over Alma's head for Bess to see her face. When she took another step, she froze and her heart began to pound.

Bess could see that the woman in the blue jeans was actually holding a pillow in her hands. She could also see that the pillow was being held, no pressed, directly onto Alma's face. She heard the woman holding the pillow breathing hard, almost as if she were crying.

"Stop!" Bess yelled.

The woman's head whipped around and something in Bess quickly thought to stop her. She could see that it was actually a young girl, maybe a teenager, holding the pillow on Alma. The girl's face was pale. She had small dark eyes that matched her long dark hair. When her eyes locked on Bess, they narrowed. Bess could see the girl was much younger and probably much stronger. She quickly threw the pillow at Bess and charged for the door.

"Help!" Bess called out. She instinctively grabbed at the girl's arm to try to stop her. Bess could feel her fingers easily wrap around the girl's narrow wrist. The girl began to heave her arm back and forth, struggling to pull away from Bess. In the struggle, Bess looked down to see a small tattoo of a cross on the girl's wrist. In that second, just as she spotted the tattoo, the girl pulled hard and managed to break away from Bess and her grip. She charged to the door and flung it open.

"Wait!" Bess called out, raising her hand in the air. Bess tried to run after the girl, but had to stop for a second to catch her breath. Standing in the doorway, Bess watched the girl's slight frame bounce down the hallway with the kind of quick easy strides that a jogger might use.

"Stop her!" Bess called out, hoping someone would hear her voice and appear in the hallway to help. The only reaction was from a white-haired lady pushing her walker down the hall. Bess knew she would not be able to catch the girl, who now slowed her stride when she turned a corner. Taking a deep breath, Bess turned and looked back at Alma.

"Oh, my dear," she said, quickly walking back to the bed.

She grabbed Alma's wrist and checked for a pulse. After a few seconds, Bess was relieved to find that one was still there. She slid her hand down from her wrist to Alma's hand and laced her fingers between Alma's fingers.

"You're okay," Bess whispered.

As she stood there next to the bed, Bess took a deep breath and tried to review the events in her mind. She tried to remember the details of the young woman's face. She made a mental note of the small black tattoo she saw on her wrist. She then sat down on the chair next to the bed and thought about what she should do next. What would a nurse say if Bess told them about the young woman attempting to smother Alma? How would a nurse react? Would they ask for evidence? Would they start to think of Bess as being confused if she could not present them with evidence? It was for these reasons that Bess knew she would have to choose her next action carefully. After all, she wouldn't be much help to Alma if she were moved to a wing of the Honey Hills Retirement Home with locked doors and supervised nursing care. Bess spent the rest of the day pondering her choices for how best to help Alma.

CLUES AND A CONCERT

The next day, Bess kept her eye on the door to Alma's room when she walked down her hallway. On occasion, she would crack the door open just enough to find Alma sleeping soundly in her bed, her covers pulled up to her neck despite the fact it was a toasty ninety degrees outside. When Bess looked in at Alma, the sight of her slumbering in bed always caused Bess to exhale with some relief. While the image of a young woman holding a pillow over Alma's face still hung in her mind, Bess was relieved to find Alma still quite well. She also kept an eye out for her at dinner time when a nurse would wheel Alma down to the dining room, park her wheelchair next to the table and help her with her food.

It was a difficult situation, Bess thought more than once while she sat in her room looking out her window. In one respect, she did want to tell someone what she saw. As was often the case in the Honey Hills Retirement Home, nurses were either too busy to listen or too skeptical to believe what they were told by the residents. Bess couldn't blame them. On occasion, she would hear some residents talk about things that didn't make sense. Things that someone of sound mind would listen to and deem crazy talk. It was that kind of reaction that Bess didn't want to spark among the nurses. Bess was of sound mind, the nurses knew it, and she didn't want to give them a reason to think otherwise.

She looked across the room at the phone. She debated about calling the police. When she first contacted them about the young man and the marijuana plant, the police would not take her seriously unless she could produce evidence of the actual plant and the person who planted it. If she were to contact them about an attempted murder, Bess could only imagine what kind of demands they would put on her before investigating. Could she describe the person? Were there any other witnesses besides herself? Did she have any physical evidence of the crime? All the questions that she knew she would have to answer with a very succinct "no."

As she weighed her choices, Bess moved her eyes across her room to her desk. She stared at the pen and paper and began to think about another option she could pursue. She got up, made her way over to her desk, scooped up the pen and slowly began to compose a note. When she finished the note, she held it up and examined what she had written. She cleared her throat and read, "I believe someone is trying to murder Alma Crisp. I walked into her room to find a young woman trying to smother Alma in her sleep with a pillow. I fear the young woman may try this again. Please keep close watch on Alma Crisp's room."

Bess paused after reading the note. She bent down to sign her name, then stopped and pulled the pen away from the paper. Perhaps, Bess thought, the note would carry more weight if the recipient did not know the name of the author.

Bess nodded in agreement with her instincts. By knowing a resident of the Honey Hills Retirement Home wrote the note, perhaps it would not be given the kind of attention that an unsigned note would. She folded the paper up and stepped into the hallway. She walked through the halls, her eyes glancing around at every face that she passed. Most were white haired residents, some nurses, a few were visitors but none fit the description of the young lady Bess encountered in Alma's room.

When she reached the office of the Director for the Honey Hills Retirement Home, Bess walked by once to see that no one was sitting at the desk. She quickly did a turn, ducked into the office, and tossed the note onto a large oak desk that belonged to the man in charge of running the Honey Hills Retirement Home. She quickly unfolded the paper and left it lying at the center of the desk.

"It would be hard to miss this," Bess said to herself and stepped out of the room.

She found a chair down the hallway where she could sit and watch the entrance to the office. It wasn't unusual to see residents of Honey Hills simply sitting and staring at the floor, the walls, or the people who walked by. Bess knew that she would not raise any suspicions by simply sitting on a chair with nothing to do.

About ten minutes later she saw a tall man wearing a blue suit and dark hair return to his office. She recognized him as being the Honey Hills Retirement Home's Director. She met him once when she was considering moving into Honey Hills. She thought from their meeting that he was a good man. Bess forgot his name, but she knew that his position was one of great authority. She watched as he stepped into his office. A few minutes went by and Bess began to grow concerned that he had missed her note on the desk. It was possible, Bess reasoned. There were other papers there. He may have quickly shuffled some papers and bumped the note right onto the floor. What was she to do if that were the case? Would she have to write another note and wait for him to leave again? Would she have to sneak into the office and place the note back onto his desk?

As she entertained each question, Bess spotted the director emerge from his office. In his hands she could see her note. He clenched the note tightly in one hand, holding it close to his face while he walked up the hall. She stood and followed him around the corner. When she tuned the corner, she saw him standing at the nurses' station, showing them the note and discussing it with them. She watched as he pointed at them and the nurses quickly pointed across their desk at the adjoining hallway. Together they quickly moved to Alma's room with Bess following behind them. When she saw them open the door and go inside, Bess simply glanced in the room to see Alma sleeping. The thought that her note had created some attention for Alma's safety made Bess smile as she walked back to her room.

Days went by, and Bess had not yet spotted the girl who had attempted to smother Alma Crisp. She roamed the hallways for days, but no face looked familiar. However, Bess was pleased that more nurses, as well as security people, were passing by Alma's room and checking up on her. After a week, Bess felt as though she needed a break from the situation.

One evening an orchestra from a local college was giving a symphony performance on the grounds of the Honey Hills Retirement Home. It was a date that Bess had marked in her calendar for months. Free ice cream and drinks would be provided for all residents who attended. Being a lover of classical music, not to mention vanilla ice cream, it was an easy choice for Bess to go.

On the evening of the show, Bess stopped by Helen Gruber's room. Helen had graduated from the college sponsoring the show. She promised Bess, over a game of bridge, that she would introduce her to the orchestra's conductor. She told Bess the conductor was a former piano student who now worked at the college as a professor of music. Bess smiled at the statement and agreed to the invitation.

When they went outside, the sky was growing dark and the clouds just above the horizon were fluffy and peach-colored. The sun was golden and round and slowly sank to the west behind a line of tall trees. Bess and Helen found a good spot under a pavilion where they quickly set up their folding chairs and began to enjoy the show.

"I flunked him," Helen announced over the music.

"What?" Bess replied, leaning closer to Helen.

"The conductor," Helen proudly stated again. "After his first month in my piano class, I flunked him."

"How do you flunk piano class?" Bess asked.

"He didn't practice," Helen explained. "I told him if he didn't make time to practice his music then I didn't care to make time for him. He came back a year later, older and more serious about his lessons. Now look at him."

Bess watched as Helen beamed with pride at her pupil, who was currently sweating while having his baton over the orchestra before him. As she listened to the symphony play, Bess decided she couldn't wait any longer. She stood up and excused herself for some ice cream. The heat of the evening, and her love of vanilla ice cream, combined to make it difficult for her to wait until intermission.

Slowly moving across the broad green yard, Bess was careful to step around the numerous rows of folding chairs that were filled with residents.

"Excuse me," Bess said with nearly every other step. It was impossible not to pass in front of someone, but she could see the table where the ice cream was being served and she could all but taste the cool vanilla flavor on her tongue.

When she finally reached the line for the ice cream, Bess folded her arms, hummed along with the music, and looked around to spot any residents she knew. Her eyes scanned many happy faces and many feet that were tapping to the rhythms. Then, quite suddenly, her eyes stopped and locked on one face she hadn't seen in a while. A face that caused her heart to race and her hands to grow quite cold.

"What kind of ice cream?" a young man asked.

Bess ignored the question and continued to stare at a young woman in the yard. The young woman stood with arms folded behind a solid row of wheelchair bound residents. Bess carefully studied the features of the young woman. She could plainly see the long black hair pulled back behind her shoulders. Bess could also see her slender arms and pale skin. Indeed, Bess was quite certain that this was the same young woman she saw in Alma's room.

Bess looked around and thought about telling someone. However, when she surveyed the hundreds of people in attendance, it didn't seem the right sort of place to accuse someone of murder. Bess knew she needed to get closer. She recalled that the young girl in question had a small tattoo of a cross on her wrist. The tattoo she saw when she grabbed the young woman's arm as she was leaving Alma's room.

"Chocolate ice cream okay?" the young man asked again.

"That's fine," Bess said, gesturing to a box of her least favorite flavor while keeping an eye on the young woman. She didn't want the woman to wander off or get lost in the crowd. She didn't want to lose her in the large swell of bodies that were sitting and walking around.

"Here you go," the young man said, handing Bess a small Styrofoam container and a narrow wooden spoon. Bess simply glanced down at them both, slipped them into her one hand, then made her way across the yard.

While she walked, Bess could barely hear the music playing. Her total focus was on getting to this young woman in a way that would not scare her off. She needed to get close to her, but not cause her to run away. She rolled the container of ice cream around in her hand while she slowly made her way down an aisle that was full of residents.

"Hi, Bess!" she heard someone call out.

"Hello," Bess called back with a wave, turning in time to see Norm and Millie Turner grinning at her from their folding chairs. In her mind, she knew they expected her to stop and join them for a lengthy conversation. She usually enjoyed talking to them and did so on more than one occasion. However, Bess continued across the yard, enduring a few more quick smiles and waves from residents she knew.

She hoped that her many friends and acquaintances wouldn't think her rude for not stopping. If so, she would one day explain to her friends how there was a young lady in attendance who had attempted to murder a dear friend. That one sentence alone, Bess reasoned, would be enough to cause anyone to forget ill-mannered behavior like not stopping to engage in chit-chat.

When she reached the row of wheelchairs where the young lady was standing, Bess quickly noticed that the young woman had positioned herself behind a wheelchair that contained none other than Alma Crisp.

"Good lord!" Bess said in a tone that was loud, but not louder than the concerto currently being played by the orchestra.

She turned and made her way down one aisle of wheelchairs. She walked in a fashion that was indistinguishable from any other resident walking around during the program. She kept her pace slow, even, and tried to remain calm as she drew closer. With each step, Bess became more and more convinced that this was the young girl she had wrestled with in Alma's room.

At about ten feet away, the young woman's head turned. Her small dark eyes looked at Bess, who quickly reacted to her icy expression with a quick smile and the decision to hold up the ice cream container in her hand.

"Ice cream for everyone, my dear," Bess managed to say in the sweetest tone of voice she could muster. She smiled and handed the container to the woman. When she reached out for it, Bess quickly caught a glance of the small black cross tattooed on her wrist. It was the same person, Bess thought. Now what was she to do?

"Are you enjoying the show?" Bess asked with a tone of voice that she tried to make both happy and care free.

"I remember you," the young woman quickly replied, her eyes lowering. She reached down to Alma's shoulder and rubbed it with one hand. "Alma told me all about you."

"Then you know what I saw?" Bess said, her tone of voice changing from light and airy to low and more direct.

"I know what you *think* you saw," the young woman stated.

"You were holding a pillow up to Alma's face when she was in bed," Bess explained in a slow and deliberate manner. "I don't think there's much room to interpret it in any other way, my dear."

"I would never kill my grandmother," the young woman quietly said.

"Your grandmother?" Bess asked, glancing down at Alma to see she was now holding the hand of the young woman.

"My name is Hannah Crisp," the young woman said. "And I know what you saw. Like I said, I would never kill my grandmother, unless…"

There was a pause in Hannah's words that led to silence. She looked down at her grandmother and said nothing.

"Unless what?" Bess finally asked.

HANNAH'S STORY

"My family lives down in Virginia," Hannah began. "My mother and father moved us down there because of my dad's job. We're the only family my grandmother has. When I had the chance to come to Pennsylvania to college I jumped at the opportunity. Grandma Crisp would always invite me up for the summer and would always make my vacations so special. I would come here to visit her whenever I could between my classes. When I'd visit we'd have lunch, play checkers, and talk about how my classes were going."

"What are you taking in college?" Bess asked.

"I hope to be a social worker," Hannah replied.

"I'm afraid they don't hire social workers who kill people," Bess quietly observed. "I think you must have a clear police record to qualify as a social worker. A friend of mine here at Honey Hills told me that once."

"Lately I've been noticing a change in my grandmother," Hannah continued, choosing to ignore what Bess had just stated. "She would ask fewer questions of me. Speak less when I came. Sometimes she'd just stare at the floor. I also noticed signs that I thought would indicate depression. I learned about depression in my psychology class. I said something to the nurses about what I saw, but they told me she was eating well and not to worry. Then Grandma Crisp started asking me a question…"

Bess watched as Hannah's eyes began to fill with tears. What she was about to say clearly made her upset and the words must have been painful to get out.

"What question, my dear," Bess urged.

"She asked if I would kill her," Hannah managed to say before breaking down. She took a few deep breaths and managed to stop her tears. "Every time I came she told me how much pain she was in. How much she wanted to die. Finally, I just decided to do what she asked, but…I don't think I could have really done it. I love her too much."

Bess wrapped her arm around Hannah's waist and felt her body jerk and move while she cried. She could also feel her shoulder growing moist as Hannah's tears poured out. It was a genuine emotion, Bess thought, not an act that was being displayed by a murderer. Now she was quite certain that Hannah was not a killer. When Bess could feel the young girl stop crying, she let go and looked Hannah in the eyes.

"You're too young to carry such burdens," Bess sighed. "Thoughts of life and death are the kinds of things that we think about here at Honey Hills. In fifty or sixty years, you may keep such weighty thoughts, but not now. College for me was all about boys and fun. Those are the thoughts that should be filling your head right now."

"And what about Grandma Crisp?" Hannah asked.

"Your grandmother's not well," Bess said, glancing down at Alma in the wheelchair. "I believe we need a doctor to help her. Together, maybe we can find a way to help her get better."

Hannah smiled and nodded. They stood silently and listened to the orchestra's final number. When it was over, Bess and Hannah were surprised to see fireworks launch high into the air. The sky filled with sparking streaks of silver, gold, red and blue. The claps of exploding fireworks traveled across the open fields of farmland and echoed off the mountain ridges that surrounded the valley. It was a spectacular sight of shimmering light that filled the sky.

Bess looked down to where Alma was sitting in her wheelchair. She walked to the front of the wheelchair, bent down and looked at Alma. She could see Alma's eyes staring straight ahead, rather than at the fireworks. Her face held no expression. Her eyes looked at Bess.

"I'm going to help you," Bess said, resting her hand on Alma's hand.

The gesture brought back memories of what she enjoyed most about working for the police. She was a police officer at a time when it meant solving an occasional crime in between serving others in the community. She worked for the police at just the right time and had good memories of helping others. As she looked at Alma, Bess hoped she would be able to help her solve this most mysterious problem.

Later that night, Bess found herself preparing for bed already eager for the morning to arrive. She had arranged for her doctor to come in and pay her a visit. She told him a few symptoms off the top of her head and then agreed to have him visit her in the morning. It would be at that point, Bess thought, that she would have him pay a visit to Alma's room instead.

As she prepared herself for bed, Alma went through the same ritual that she had done for her nearly eighty years of life. She removed her jewelry and carefully placed it in the same jewelry box she had received from her father when she turned sixteen. The two ballet dancers that adorned the side of the box, while faded, still greeted her with a smile every evening. Next, she brushed her hair twenty times as her mother had advised back when her hair was darker and more flowing. This was followed by a trip to the sink to wash her face and brush her teeth. She still brushed her teeth with the same approach that her dentist advised when she was just a little girl. Finally, she sat on her bed and opened her family Bible.

In between the pages of the Book of Luke, her husband's favorite book of the Bible, there were some white locks of hair. They were locks that Bess had cut from her husband's head just before they closed his casket and laid him to rest. As she had done since they were married, Bess always gently stroked her husband's hair with her finger tips before she went to sleep. After a few seconds she whispered,

"Good night, my love," before closing the book and climbing into bed.

Tonight while she lay in bed, Bess thought about the events of the day. She thought about Alma and hoped all would be well for her tonight. She could feel her eyes grow heavy as she began to think about Hannah, and how difficult it must be to have someone you love ask you to kill them. If her husband had done the same thing at the height of his pain from cancer, would Bess have acted much differently than Hannah? The question caused Bess to think for just a few more minutes before she could feel herself slowly begin to drift off to sleep.

In the final moments before sleep, the moments when one can hear any sound and sense any presence, Bess thought she heard a baby. It wasn't a cry, but rather a coo or babbling sound that she seemed to be hearing. Her eyes were now closed and she was nearly wrapped in that warm familiar blanket of sleep. It had been a long time since she had dreams about her baby. She hoped that the dreams weren't going to begin again.

CLOUDS IN THE STOMACH

The next morning, Bess wrote a note, taped it to the outside of her door, then left her room and closed the door behind her. It was not unusual to leave notes on the doors at Honey Hills. Some residents had added small chalkboards or writing pads for people to leave notes in case they came to visit. While Bess didn't feel a need to be concerned with missing visitors, this morning was different. She turned around and looked at the name on the note and hoped that the person for whom the note was written would come soon.

Bess wandered down the hallway to Alma's room. Most mornings, Bess would quietly open the door a crack, peak her head in to check on Alma before going to breakfast. This morning, she grabbed hold of the door handle and pushed the door wide open. There she found Alma still in bed, white sheet up to her neck, her eyes open and staring out the window.

"Good morning, Alma," Bess said, stepping close to the bed.

Alma's eyes turned towards Bess, then turned back outside. Bess walked over to a dresser filled with framed photographs. There she saw pictures of a younger Alma standing next to a dark haired man in a suit that she guessed was Alma's husband. Some more pictures featured Alma and her children, back when they were all younger and looked happy. A few pictures were of Alma when she was older, standing with her now grown-up children and grandchildren. Bess leaned close and could even make out the smiling face of Hannah standing next to Alma. The happy faces of Alma and Hannah indicated to Bess that this was a picture clearly taken during better times. In the last two days, Bess had yet to see either Alma or Hannah do much smiling.

"Why are you here, Bess?" Alma finally spoke with a quivering voice.

"You know, Alma," Bess began. "I met your granddaughter the other day. The one that comes here and visits you."

"Hannah?" Alma asked.

"Yes," Bess quietly answered.

"Hmm," Alma grunted and looked back out the window.

"Such a nice girl, Hannah," Bess began, stepping back towards the bed. "She said you asked her to kill you? She's such a sweet girl. Why would you ask her to do such a thing?"

"You shouldn't ask such questions," Alma mumbled.

"You know," Bess continued, "when my husband was undergoing treatment for cancer, he was in tremendous pain. He asked me more than once to let him die. It was the hardest thing I ever did in my life watching my husband in so much pain. I really did want him to die, but I knew it was not right to take such decisions in my own hand. I was much older than Hannah and was able to deal with such emotions. You can't put a lovely young girl like Hannah in that kind of position. Tell me, Alma, do you really want to die?"

"Yes," Alma replied without hesitation.

"You didn't last month at Bingo," Bess recalled. "Do you remember how you cheered when you won the big prize for the night? You actually stood on your chair and waved to every-one with a wonderful smile. You weren't thinking about dying then, so why would you want to die now?"

She watched Alma's eyes drift away from the window. She grew silent and stared at her bed linens for minute. Bess began to wonder if she would get an answer or not.

"Is it sunny today?" Alma asked.

"Yes," Bess answered, looking outside. "It's a beautiful summer day out there."

"It doesn't *feel* sunny," Alma sighed. She sat up in her bed just a little, made a fist and put it on her chest. "In here, every day feels cloudy. Rainy. Depressing. I know it's summer. I know the sun is out a lot. I just cannot take another day of feeling like this. Feeling like I've got a stomach full of rain and clouds and storms and darkness. Feeling like I've got a belly full of things that are making me sad. I just want someone to crack me open and let all the bad things out. Have you ever felt that way, Bess?"

As Bess thought about her answer, there was a knock on the door. Bess turned just in time to see the door open and a balding, white haired man appear. He had round black glasses and was carrying a small black bag. The man smiled when he entered and looked right at Bess.

"Good morning, Doctor Goodman," Bess quickly said.

"Good morning, Bess," Doctor Goodman replied, walking over to Alma's bed. "I believe we have an appointment for this morning. I got the note on your door and came here right away. Shall we return to your room?"

"In a moment," Bess replied, turning her eyes to Alma. "I was a little concerned about my friend, doctor. She doesn't seem to have any real physical problems, but she has been having more and more trouble coping with some kind of depression. Is that usually related to any physical illnesses you are aware of?"

"Let me see," Doctor Goodman said. He adjusted his glasses, stepped up to the bed and looked into Alma's eyes. He put both hands around her face, then squeezed a few times down the sides of her neck. While he checked her there was a knock on the door. Bess turned to see the nurse coming in with three small paper cups.

"Excuse me, doctor," the nurse said in a polite tone. "It's time for Alma's medicine this morning."

Bess noticed how the doctor's eyes quickly surveyed the pills in the three cups. He snatched the cups from the nurse and walked over to the dresser. He dumped the pills out on the table and began to inspect them.

"Doctor!" the nurse snapped.

"Do you know what she's taking?" Doctor Goodman asked.

"What?" the nurse asked, clearly confused.

"Her meds," Doctor Goodman said. "What kind of medication is she taking?"

"I...I'd have to check her charts," the nurse confessed.

"I'll tell you what you'll find," Doctor Goodman said. He held two pills, one green and one blue, in his hand. He dropped them into the nurse's hand and pointed to her. "You run these down to the pharmacy. Ask them to see if they should be given in combination. I think you might learn that these pills, when taken together, will cause some depression as a side effect. Tell the pharmacist that there are other pills that will do the same things, but not cause the depression. How long has she been taking these?"

"She's been on them about three weeks," the nurse replied. "The day Alma started on the blue pills was my birthday. That's how I know for sure."

"Well then she needs a more competent doctor!" Doctor Goodman snapped, squeezing the pills in his hand.

There it was, three weeks, just about the time all of the signs appeared. The quieter person in the dining hall for meals. Alma's requests for her dear granddaughter to commit murder. The unkempt look and dress. It amazed Bess how one's whole being could be altered or changed in some way by something as small as a pill.

"Now," Doctor Goodman said, "back to my original patient. Bess let's go back to your room and talk about that shortness of breath you were describing to me over the phone."

"Yes, doctor," Bess replied. She smiled to herself as she watched the nurse slip the pills back into their cups and back onto the cart. Bess gently put her hand on Alma's hand, leaned close to her and whispered,

"You're going to feel better, Alma. Those little pills you've been taking have been filling you up with those storm clouds. You'll be feeling better real soon."

For the first time in a long time, Bess Bullock saw a smile come across the face of Alma Crisp. It was the first smile she'd seen in a month and it made Bess feel as if she were walking on air. As she left the room with Doctor Goodman, Bess tried to keep her smile from growing too wide. After all, since he had helped Alma as Bess had hoped, Bess now needed to pretend to be a little sick so Doctor Goodman didn't suspect otherwise.

A week later, it was Bingo night. The evening was popular among the residents at the Honey Hills Retirement Home because of the prizes that were usually offered. As Bess saw it, no money was required to play and if the Bingo chips fell into the right places one could win a box of candy, or tissues, or even a bag of cough drops. It was a good way of earning something for nothing, Bess concluded, despite the fact that she only came on occasion.

While Bess sat, arranging her Bingo cards and her Bingo chips, she scanned the hall at the two distinct types of faces that were present in the room. She laughed at the serious faces who were usually in attendance for the sole purpose of accumulating things or for the competition of winning. She also spotted the smiling faces, those residents who came to be part of something fun and share in good conversation. As she looked at all the faces, Bess stopped and could feel her smile broaden and the wrinkles around her cheeks push up. There, she saw Alma and Hannah Crisp, sitting together, laughing about something while they laid out their Bingo cards and munched on some punch and cookies. If there were any prize Bess would take away from tonight's Bingo, no prize would be any greater than the image she had of Alma and Hannah. Clearly, Bess thought, there were no storm clouds or rain to be found around Alma. Just a genuine smile and love for her granddaughter.

A CONSTANT SKY

Later that night Bess found herself in the unusual position of being unable to sleep. Normally, she nodded off the second her head hit the pillow. However, the details of Alma's case were fresh in her mind. The excitement of resolving the mystery pumped through her body. She tossed and turned in her sheets until midnight, then decided to slip on her robe and take a walk. She grabbed a large book from her nightstand and opened the door to her room. She paused in the doorway, careful to look in both directions before walking into the empty hallway. Quietly she moved, careful to peak around corners for any approaching nurses. She didn't feel up to entertaining questions about why she was walking in the hallways at midnight. She wasn't even interested in any type of conversation about why she was carrying a book or where she was going to read at such a late hour.

After going down a few hallways, Bess finally reached an exit door. She opened the door and slowly stepped outside into the darkness. Bess was keenly aware that the door would lock if she let it close. She bent down and laid the book in between the door and the frame, allowing the door to rest against it.

Finally outside, Bess found a bench and sat down. The air was slightly warmer than inside the Honey Hills Retirement Home, but more humid. The sounds of a late summer night were entertaining for Bess to hear. There was a virtual concerto of crickets at work tonight. Some maintained low humming sounds that were strong and

steady. Other crickets were higher pitched, chirping off
and on with a consistent regularity. A few crickets seldom
chirped, but when they did it was in a high rich tone that
overwhelmed the other crickets' sounds.

Bess finally turned her mind away from what she
heard to what she saw. She tilted her head up to the sky
and peered into the patches of stars that spread out above
her.

"Retirement," Bess sighed.

She quite enjoyed solving Alma's mystery. It felt
good to have her instincts lead her through each turn along
the way. Yet, she was nearly eighty. Perhaps this would
be her last mystery to solve. Despite what her mind and
instincts told her, maybe her body was ready to slip into an
easy routine of cards, books, and other leisure activities. Is
that what retirement was going to be for Bess? Days of
resting her body, but still engaging her mind?

"Why do we have to grow old?" Bess sighed to the
stars.

She recognized some of the stars from her
childhood years. She spotted Orion the Hunter and
Cassiopeia, two of her favorites. Part of her liked the
elegance of being a queen while another part liked the idea
of being a hunter and using her instincts to track and
capture something. Not all the stars in the sky held a story.
Some stars lay by themselves, burning quite brightly and
demanding attention because of their luminous glow.
Living in the country, with no major city lights, Bess loved
the clarity of a night sky.

"Is this what you looked like eighty years ago?"
Bess whispered to the stars.

Indeed, it was soon going to be her birthday. In
about a week, Bess was going to turn eighty. She was quite
proud of this achievement. Everything in her body told her
this was an achievement worthy of a special celebration.
This was the thought that had kept her awake and led her

outside at such a late hour. What special thing could she do to mark this milestone?

She sat quietly, staring up at the dark sky and the peerless points of light and began to realize that if anything had remained the same since the day of her birth it was the sky. Cities changed. People changed. Even land she knew as a child had been changed for the construction of houses or towns. Yet, the sky was the one constant. It was the one thing that had never changed.

"Perhaps the sky would be the perfect place to celebrate a birthday," Bess quietly said to herself. She sat back on the bench, continuing to look up, and began to contemplate the meaning behind her words. As she sat, she could hear a low humming sound in the distance. Her eyes moved around before finding one small piece of light that was moving across the sky. Suddenly, as if the answer had dropped from the stars, Bess had found her answer.

"Of course," she said to herself.

With that thought, Bess suddenly stood up and went back inside. She made her way back to her room thankful that tomorrow would be Tuesday. She was anxious to share her idea for a special birthday with her friends. Settling back into her bed, sleep came a bit more easily.

The next morning, Bess waited the conversation around the bridge table centered around Bess and what she had done to save Alma. Helen, Rose and Flo spoke with louder voices and their eyes looked a bit wider than usual. They were clearly excited with what Bess had done to save Alma.

"You must be very excited about it all," Rose said, her eyes shifting away from her cards to Bess. "She owes you her life, you know. I mean…Alma is lucky you were there to save her."

"Very lucky," Flo echoed from behind her cards.

Bess nodded at the comments but didn't say anything. Was this retirement? Breaking up a murder attempt? Was this going to help Bess rid herself of her police instincts? Was this going to help her fill her days with idle time? Bess shifted in her seat. The questions in her mind made her feel a bit uncomfortable. She looked around at the faces of her friends and forced a more pleasant thought into her head.

"I've decided what I'd like to do for my birthday," Bess announced.

"Is it your birthday?" Rose asked, lowering her cards.

"How old are you?" Flo chimed in.

"I'll be turning eighty in a few days," Bess announced. "I've decided I would like to go up for a flight in an airplane."

"You want to what?" Flo laughed, nearly dropping her cards.

"You heard me," Bess replied, her eyes narrowing at Flo's expression. "It's my birthday and I want to do something special. I want to do something more than sit in this place and let them bring me a birthday cake after dinner. I've seen that happen to other residents and it wouldn't make me the least bit happy to hear a weak chorus of "Happy Birthday" after supper. I want to do something special. Something…that will make my heart feel like it's going to grow wings and fly!" "But why an airplane?" Rose pressed. "Just seems like an odd choice."

"I thought about a balloon," Bess said, "but the farm country is just so pretty. I want to see it all from up above. I think an airplane would be a nice way to see all the farms that are in the valley. What a better way to start a birthday morning than having a view like that."

Silence greeted her enthusiastic words. Bess cleared her throat and sat up straight. She looked around at her friends' faces and then threw out a question she had pondered all morning.

"Who wants to go with me?"

Again, silence was the only response that answered her question.

"Come on, ladies!" Bess finally spoke up. "I'm paying for the plane. I don't think it would be such a big deal to have one of you join me. It wouldn't be much fun going by myself."

"My doctor told me to avoid stress," Flo said in a clear and loud tone. "Going up in a plane would just make me too nervous, Bess."

"I've never been on a plane," Rose announced with a shake of her head. "I don't intend to start now."

"How about you, Helen?" Bess asked, turning to the last person at the table.

"I'm like Flo," Helen announced, twirling a few strands of her hair. "I take blood pressure medicine, Bess. I don't think it would be a very good idea for me to go up in a plane. I think I should call my doctor first."

"No, no," Bess said with a wave of her hand. She stood up at the table and looked around. "You don't understand. I don't want any of you to do this because your doctor said it was okay, or because you're trying to conquer some fear. I want you to do it because you're excited about trying something different."

"Well," Rose said, looking at Flo and Helen, "I guess we're the wrong people to ask to try something different. Some of us enjoy our quiet days. We don't need to ride in an airplane to make our days enjoyable."

"Why don't you have your daughter go with you," Helen suggested.

"Samantha?" Bess laughed. "She doesn't even know about this. If I told her how much money I was paying to ride in a plane, she wouldn't be able to sit back and enjoy it."

The room grew silent again. Bess could sense some tension in the air. In one respect, there was the obligation one felt to take up the invitation of a friend. In another respect, there was the obligation one had for good health and self-preservation. Judging by the looks on the faces of her friends, Bess could tell they were torn by both choices.

"You're my friends," Bess stated with a smile. "I just thought it would be fun for all of us to go together on this plane ride. I suppose I just expected too much from each of you. I tend to do that sometimes with people. In my mind, I'll see how I think things should be and then I have to deal with disappointment when things turn out differently."

"Sorry, Bess," Rose said and she reached out and patted Bess on the arm with her hand.

"We're not adventure seekers," Flo mumbled. "That's why we live here. Couldn't we just buy you a present at the gift shop and sing to you in your room?"

"A present would be nice," Bess nodded, "but it just wouldn't make my heart fly."

As she watched the cards move across the table, and listened to her friends speak about her offer, Bess began to wonder if this was all her friends were capable of. Were they merely here to offer kind words and not kind actions? Was she meant to spend her birthday alone in her airplane?

BREAD IN THE BASKET

One thing that made Bess feel a bit more at home in the Honey Hills Retirement Home was the presence of bread at the dinner table. It was a little thing, and she knew it, but sometimes it was an abundance of little things that made the difference in how one felt about something. In this case coming to a dinner table with a clear stack of sliced bread on a dish, accompanied by butter, was one thing that made her transition to Honey Hills a bit more familiar.

Growing up, it was her father who always had a stack of bread on his plate next to his meal. As a young girl, Bess thought her father silly for eating bread with every meal. It was as if, she recalled, he was trying to make a sandwich out of every thing they had for dinner. When she grew older her tastes began to vary. Her father pointed out how bread could be used to conceal the flavors of foods she didn't like but had to eat. When her mother put a spoonful of spinach on her plate, Bess would reach for the bread. When her mother made liver and onions, her father's favorite, Bess would reach for the bread. As the years went by, Bess found herself having a slice of bread with every meal, regardless of the food.

When it came to meals in the Honey Hills Retirement Home's dining hall, Bess sat at the same table, with the same ladies, for breakfast, lunch and dinner. Fortunately, she was the only one of the four who ate bread. Sometimes, depending on the quality of her food, or the spices added to it, Bess would have three slices of bread to consume with her meal. Since she was usually the only one at her table to have bread with her dinner, there was always a healthy supply on hand for her to eat. However, over the last few days she was beginning to see a change in the amount of bread that was available to her.

While she tended to focus on her plate and her food when she ate, Bess began to observe that the bread dish was growing empty at a much faster rate. It was just a little thing. A small observation that the other ladies at the table were oblivious to. Yet, after months of recognizing the eating habits of each woman at the table, Bess was now faced with the strange question of finding out which person's eating habits had changed. Who was eating more bread?

One evening Bess decided to keep her head up and focus less on the food. When the server brought Bess a dinner consisting of a small dish of pears, a small bowl of green peas, a larger dish of chicken pot pie, and a drink, Bess thanked the server and looked around. She scooped up some bites and watched the other ladies at the table begin to eat. Her eyes moved from side to side, watching each person consume their food while she did the same.

"Did you have a good day?" Dawn Smithson asked from across the table.

"Yes, I did," Bess responded. It was the same response she gave to anyone who would ask that question. Soft music, three meals, and air conditioning made every day a good one for Bess.

Half way through the meal, Bess looked around the table. She could see half a slice of bread on Dawn Smithson's plate. She also could see that Minnie Quill, sitting to the right of Bess, did not take any bread. A terribly thin woman, Bess often thought she could use a slice or two. As the meal continued, Bess turned to her left. There she saw Charlotte Lapp, an older Mennonite woman, with two pieces of bread resting on her plate. Bess also could see the crust of a slice of bread under Charlotte's napkin. Bess stared at the empty bread plate. Having already consumed two slices, she was quite full. Yet, she was curious why Charlotte was hiding a slice of bread in her napkin.

"Excuse me," Bess spoke up, lowering her eyes down to her plate. "Could you pass the bread please?"

"I'm afraid there's none left," Charlotte quickly answered.

Bess directed her eyes to Charlotte's napkin and the slice of bread tucked under it. She then saw Charlotte reach over with her other hand and take one of the two slices of bread from her plate and hand it to Bess.

"Here," she said. "You can have mine. I'm not going to eat it."

"Thank you, Charlotte," Bess said, carefully taking the bread from her hand.

Why, Bess thought, would she hand me a slice of bread from her plate when there was a perfectly good piece of bread in her napkin? The way she ate her dinner, Bess found it hard to believe that Charlotte was actually going to be hungry for two more slices of bread.

In the previous months, Bess knew Charlotte as the one person at the table who ate half of everything. Half of her meats, vegetables, fruit, even the occasional slice of pie. She was never one to ask for seconds. She was also never one to have a clear plate. Yet, here she was, concealing food in a napkin for reasons that Bess was not quite sure about. It was this question that Bess entertained for the rest of the evening.

She thought about it as she walked around the hallways, standing at various windows to get better views of the sun as it descended into a puddle of gold just beyond the horizon. She thought about it when she sat in front of the TV staring at a screen of young people she didn't know on a TV show she never really watched all that much. Her instincts as a detective were like an itch that she had to fight to resist.

"No," Bess quietly spoke to her instincts.

She drew in her breath and changed for bed. She turned out the light in her room, and climbed into bed. Bess did the same thing she always did before going to sleep. She thanked God for the day, for helping her live a good life, and asked God to take care of her dear husband.

As she closed her eyes, and slowly began to drift off to sleep, Bess started to hear the sounds of a baby again. It was the second night in a row she heard such sounds before falling asleep. She kept her eyes closed, remained in the darkness and let her mind race to a memory from many years ago. A memory of her and her husband holding a very small baby.

When Bess was pregnant for the second time, her son was born prematurely. She could still hear the doctors tell her the child only had a few hours to live. In those few hours, Bess made a point of holding him close and saying his name over and over.

"Adam. Your name is Adam. I am your mother and you are my Adam."

She could still see his small eyes stay closed. His small hand rested on her finger. She wanted him to know his name before he left this life. She knew he was too young to understand, but even if he remembered her voice, it gave her some comfort before he returned to the company of angels. The next morning, she had to tell young Samantha that her baby brother went to heaven to play with the angels and that she wouldn't be a big sister.

For many years after that night, Bess would have dreams of Adam. In her dreams, she would hear his cries and wake up in a cold sweat, then cry herself. It had been many years since she had such dreams. Many years since she woke up in tears. Were the dreams beginning again?

Was Adam trying to contact her? The thought caused her to sit straight up in bed.

"Adam," she said, reaching for her glasses and fumbling for the light.

When she turned on the light she realized she was now fully awake. She now knew she wasn't dreaming, but she could still hear the sound of a baby's voice. She slid off her bed and into her slippers. As she stood, she could hear both her knees crack as they always did when she got up from her bed. She liked to think that they were the only things in the world that consistently greeted her to another day. She slipped on a white robe and matching slippers, then made her way for the door to find the source of the baby's voice.

She didn't like going into the hallway this late at night. The halls were dim and silent. In her mind, there was a clear difference between quiet and silent. During the day time, there were people walking around the halls, not saying much or speaking in quiet tones. This late at night the silence in the hallways reflected the fact that there were no people around. Yet, she could hear the faint sound of a woman's voice humming a song. Bess looked left, then right, then moved in the direction of the woman's voice. She walked to her neighbor's door, where she could hear Charlotte Lapp singing.

Standing in front of Charlotte's door, Bess paused for moment. It was late and she felt ridiculous for knocking on the door at this hour. Then, she heard the sound of a baby's voice followed closely by the sound of Charlotte's voice. Bess made a fist to knock on the door, then stopped and lowered her hand. In her mind, Bess recalled how Charlotte so cleverly used her napkin to conceal the slice of bread at dinner. Perhaps she would try to do the same thing with the baby if Bess knocked on the door. Perhaps she would try to conceal the child, or simply block the door so Bess wouldn't be able to come in. These thoughts led her hand to the door knob, where Bess took a firm grasp of the handle and turned it.

When the door opened, she saw Charlotte on her rocking chair. She was wearing a blue robe and a white night gown under the robe. She was also holding a small baby on her lap. The child looked to be about one year old, Bess guessed. The baby's blonde hair was highlighted by a lamp next to her rocker. She watched the baby's blue eyes focus on her, and Bess couldn't help but smile.

"Close that door!" Charlotte snapped with a sharp tone that made Bess jump.

Bess quickly did as she was told. She then took a few steps towards Charlotte and pointed at the baby. The baby giggled at Bess and without a conscious thought, Bess wiggled her finger and tickled the baby's foot.

"Who is this?" Bess asked.

"My grandson, Jonah," Charlotte replied. "I'm sorry if he woke you, Bess. I was afraid he was being too loud. Only a matter of time before you found out about him I guess."

"Charlotte," Bess smiled, stepping closer. "He is just the most beautiful little baby. Who does he belong to?"

"My daughter," Charlotte answered, jingling some keys in front of the child. Jonah grabbed the keys from Charlotte's hand and shook them.

"You know we're not permitted to have guests overnight," Bess said. "I'd suppose that rule does include babies."

"I know," Charlotte replied.

"Why is he..." Bess began.

"My daughter does not have the best taste in men," Charlotte explained. "Her boyfriend, Jonah's father, was arrested for drugs here not so long ago. She said he was growing a plant right out there in the courtyard that he was going to use for making drugs. Someone found out, called the police and now he's in prison waiting to go before a judge. My daughter thinks he'll get probation, but she needs to get a second job to pay her rent while she waits for her boyfriend to get out. She has a friend who watches Jonah during the day. Her second job requires her to work at night, which means I get to have little Jonah here with me for a few hours."

A tremendous wave of guilt fell over Bess. She was the one who had made that phone call and reported the boyfriend. At the time, it seemed like such a correct decision to make. A clear case of what was right and wrong to her. Looking at Charlotte with her little grandson, Bess could feel her heart ache. Here was this little child, an innocent in the world, whose father was involved with drugs and whose mother had to work so hard that the baby wasn't around her all that much. What a way to start off in this life, Bess thought.

"So this is our little bread eater?" Bess asked.

"I knew you saw the bread in my napkin," Charlotte laughed. "Yes, I have found that some bread fills Jonah up quite nicely in the evening. A full belly helps him fall to sleep. My daughter picks him up very late at night and slips out the exit door around the corner from my room. We have to be careful of the nurses, you know, so it helps if Jonah's sleeping when I give him to his mother."

Charlotte grew silent, her eyes drifted down to Jonah who was quietly playing with her keys. He let out a yawn, rubbed one of his eyes, then let the keys drop to the floor. He rubbed his small hands along the sleeve of Charlotte's robe and yawned again.

"Are you going to tell?" Charlotte asked while kissing the top of Jonah's blond head. Bess lowered her eyes. She walked over to a chair next to where Charlotte was sitting. She folded her arms and looked down at the floor.

"You know," Bess began. "When I walk around this place and I see all of the mothers that roam these hallways, I often think there is something missing here. We all have these feelings and instincts buried inside of us from long ago when we had our children. We all had babies. We all loved our babies. Just when we got good at feedings and diapers and cuddling and reading books to our babies, God makes them grow up. Then we are left with all these feelings as mothers that we have no one to shower them upon."

"Are you going tell?" Charlotte asked again.

"No," Bess quickly answered. "Your secret is safe with me, Charlotte. I can't think of a better place for little Jonah to be than with you."

"Good," Charlotte answered. She looked at Jonah and smiled. "I think he quite likes it here. It's quieter than his apartment in the city. At least that's what his mother tells me."

Charlotte stood up, holding Jonah in both hands. She took a few steps and leaned over to Bess, who instinctively held out her arms. Charlotte handed her Jonah. The second she touched his soft clothes Bess could feel her heart skip a beat.

"I've got to use the bathroom," Charlotte said. She looked at Jonah and smiled. "Be right back, sweetie."

When the door to the bathroom slowly closed, Bess now found herself in unfamiliar territory. She hadn't been alone in a room with a baby since she held her son. Still there was something about it all that just felt comfortable and familiar. How the baby's head rested in her arm. How his brown eyes looked up at her from time to time. She ran her hand over his small white pajama shirt and looked at the small red truck on it.

"Truck?" Bess whispered, pointing to his shirt. "You like trucks?"

Jonah looked at her and she thought he was trying to smile.

"Or do you just like me to tickle your belly?" Bess asked, poking him gently with her finger. Jonah smiled and then made a sound that she thought to be a giggle. The sound of a child's laugher, Bess thought, was as close as she would come to the fountain of youth. She closed her eyes and nuzzled her nose against the top of Jonah's wispy dark hair. She could feel the warmth of his head. She could also smell the sweet scents that always seemed to accompany a baby. Each time she filled herself with the smells of Jonah, Bess felt like she was thirty-three again, leaving the police force to stay home and raise her family. Bess stood quietly with young Jonah, savoring each second before Charlotte returned. She savored the seconds that she felt like a mother.

SINCERITY AND BLUE EYES

Within a few days of moving to the Honey Hills Retirement Home, Bess quickly noticed that there were more women than men present. Bess often thought that while most of the women she spoke with had spent their lives raising their children, the men were not so fortunate. Most husbands of her generation had to spend their years working hard to provide for their families. Her husband was one of them.

Bess recalled more than once how her husband had in fact spent a good many years working hard in the local steel foundry. For his years working and forging steel, he was able to provide a good living for the family. However, in being a wonderful provider, there were some little sacrifices that Bess could clearly remember.

Holding hands was one of those sacrifices. When they were young and dating, she recalled how much they loved to hold hands. How their fingers laced perfectly together. For Bess, it was a sign that they were meant to be together. However, when he began working at the steel foundry, holding hands would become something they wouldn't do as often.

As his years of employment at the steel foundry grew, so did the size of his hand. Bess noticed how the palms of his hands, once soft, grew tougher and developed a leathery quality. She also began to see that his fingers were growing thicker from his years of handling steel. It was not the same hand she once held when they were young and dating. Now it was a hand that had grown tough over time. When her husband died, his hand was the last thing she touched before closing his casket.

This morning, she was thinking about hands while she attended a meeting of the Honey Hills Waltzing Club. She enjoyed dancing since she was a girl. She and her husband would only dance together at weddings. She would have liked to dance more, but with raising Samantha and having a husband not inclined to dance, Bess simply put her passion on hold. Shortly after she moved into the Honey Hills Retirement Home, Bess knew she wanted to attend the Waltzing Club meetings being offered. Aside from Bridge Club, it was another morning she looked forward to each week.

"Good morning, Fancy Feet," Chet Wooden joked whenever Bess entered the ballroom. Chet was the president of the club. A kind man well into his eighties, Chet always had a welcome smile for Bess. His blue eyes held a glimmer in them when she saw him. Early on when they first met they discovered common ground in that they had both lost their spouses to cancer. When they discovered a mutual love for dancing, Chet and Bess became fast friends.

"Ready to swing with the music this morning?" Chet asked.

"Oh, yes," Bess replied. "Dancing is what I look forward to. You know it's my favorite day of the week. Everyone should have something to look forward to during the week, don't you agree? How sad life would be without things to look forward to."

"Well said, Bess," Chet replied.

In the moments that followed, Chet went on to explain to Bess and the other eight people in attendance what type of dancing they would do today. He also told them what type of music they would be using to accompany the dance. Then, when he finished, Chet pressed a button on a CD player and waved Bess over to him.

Together they stepped out on the dance floor with the other couples. The music echoed throughout the room as Bess and Chet danced to the rhythms. With each step, Chet kept a smile off his face and remained totally focused. Bess liked Chet because he was so sincere about everything he did. He spoke softly, had a big heart, and only smiled when he meant it.

This was the quality that Bess found so attractive about Chet. Most people, it seemed to Bess, used a smile like a form of punctuation. They would add it to the end of a sentence, a story, or a comment. If Bess didn't agree with what another person said, she still felt as though it was harder to express her disagreement when the other person smiled. With Chet, Bess didn't feel compelled to follow such social mores. He was a straightforward man who spoke what he thought and let people know where he stood on things.

Something else she liked was how he held her hand when they danced. He didn't grab her tightly. He didn't hold her hand with a strong grip. He gently cradled her hand in his when they danced. His hands reminded her of her late husband's hands before he worked at the steel foundry. They were soft and just the right size for Bess to lace her fingers around. Perhaps, she thought, this was the real reason she enjoyed her dance club so much. Perhaps, she guessed, it was not because of dancing but because of being able to hold hands again. Of course, she would be too embarrassed to say anything like this to Chet. She guessed he would also be too embarrassed to hear such comments. So when they weren't on the dance floor, Chet and Bess simply enjoyed each other's company from time to time around the Honey Hills Retirement Home. On occasion they would pass in the hallway and smile. However, Bess chose not to do more than that. She wouldn't stop him in the hallway and begin a conversation. No, Bess was quite content in knowing that one day out of the week was their day to be alone, just the two of them on the dance floor.

One morning, after they finished dancing, Bess was sitting on a chair when she saw Chet walk over to her. He sat down beside her, breathing slightly hard after they finished dancing. His cheeks and the tip of his nose were bright red. He wiped the perspiration from his forehead with a handkerchief and sniffed.

"You told me once you were a pilot during World War II," Bess said.

"That's right," Chet answered.

"Do you like flying?" Bess asked.

"Loved it!" Chet quickly answered. "Couldn't think of a better place to be than in the sky. Why do you ask?"

"No reason," Bess said, her eyes turning away. The few seconds of silence that followed were a bit awkward. Bess wasn't sure if she should explain her line of questioning or not. Should she share her idea for celebrating her birthday? Would Chet be interested in flying with her?

"Bess," Chet finally spoke. "Since we're talking about our pasts, someone told me that you used to work for the police. Is that true?"

"Yes," Bess quietly answered. It was the first time he talked to her about something other than dancing, which took her by surprise.

"Would you ever investigate crimes?" he asked.

"On occasion," Bess said, leaning back in her seat and taking a moment to think about the question. "Back then, crimes were different than they are today. I sit in my room some nights watching the news and I hear about all the murders and shootings and I'm thankful I'm not with the police today. Why do you ask?"

"Because there have been some crimes being committed around here," Chet answered.

His words caused Bess to lean forward. She could feel her back straighten and her eyes grow a little wider.

"Go on," she said, adjusting her silver hair with her hand.

"Last night," Chet began. "I was getting ready for bed and I emptied my pockets onto a small table next to my bed. My keys and my wallet and any loose change in my pockets always get dropped on that little table before I go to sleep. When I woke up this morning, I found that my wallet was gone and the door to my room had been left open. Now my wallet is fairly large. It's leather and black and filled with things like pictures of my family and some money. I just can't believe that someone would come into my room and take it during the night."

"I can't imagine it either," Bess said, her heart racing just slightly. She thought for a moment that she would need her heart medication, then realized it was just the excitement of a mystery being revealed to her.

"You pay all that money to get into a place like this," Chet complained, "and you still can't get away from the problems of the world."

"Well, Chet," Bess smiled. "They didn't nail the front door shut when we came here to live. Visitors do come and go."

"But not that late at night," Chet observed. "They lock the doors after ten o'clock. My wallet was there when I went to sleep at eleven o'clock."

"So you think it was someone who lives here?" Bess asked.

Chet quietly nodded. He adjusted the glasses on his sloped nose and wiped his forehead again with the back of his hand.

"I'm not that good at going around asking questions," he explained. "I thought maybe you'd be better at it than me. You know, since you've had all that practice from being a police officer, I just thought you'd be better at finding clues."

"I see," Bess said. "Have you told the nurses about this?"

"Yes," Chet replied. "They told me I must have misplaced it. You know how they are, Bess. Every time we have a problem, the nurses think it must be because of our age. That makes me feel very humiliated sometimes."

"Me too," Bess added, even though she had not experienced something like that yet.

She reached her hand over to Chet's hand. He flipped the palm of her hand over and covered it with his larger hand. He looked at her and gave her that genuine smile that she always felt was like a window to his heart.

"I   will   help   you,"   she   quietly   promised.

Together they quietly sat for a moment, there hands and fingers softly resting together.

The next day, Bess made her way to the dining hall for breakfast. She had her usual, a small bow of cereal and one banana, along with a glass of juice. With little variations here or there, she had always eaten the same thing for breakfast for the last thirty years. Some people might call it a rut, but Bess looked at it from a very simple vantage point: It tasted good and she liked having it for breakfast.

After breakfast, she went down to the hallway where Chet lived. She could quickly feel that it was warmer in the hall, and guessed the air conditioning was broken. There were seven other rooms in this hallway. Chet's room made it eight, four on each side. Bess took a deep breath, walked up to the door across the hall from Chet's room and knocked. The force of her knock actually caused the door to open, revealing a woman sitting in a chair, bare feet propped up, holding a magnifying glass in her hand to read the newspaper.

"Do I know you?" the woman asked.

"I'm sorry for opening your door," Bess apologized.

"It's okay," the woman replied, "that door never latches when I close it. I've talked to maintenance about it. They say the wood doors are swelled from the heat and humidity. I can't wait for that air conditioning to be fixed. What did you say your name was?"

"I'm a friend of your neighbor, Chet," Bess answered. "I live in the other wing. In hallway number seven. My name is Bess Bullock."

"Any friend of Chet's is a friend of mine," the woman smiled. "He's just such a pleasant person, don't you think?"

"Yes," Bess nodded. "All though he's not too pleasant right now. Seems that someone took his wallet last night while he was sleeping."

"Really?" the woman replied, lowering the magnifying glass from her face. "Someone came in and took his wallet? Last night?"

"That's what Chet says," Bess replied. "Do you remember hearing anything last night."

"No," the woman replied. She gestured to her ear with her finger and smiled. "I usually don't wear my hearing aid to bed, though. That's why I sleep so well."

The woman cleared her throat and struggled to her feet. She took very small steps and shuffled over to where Bess was standing. When she stopped, Bess could make out the sweet smell of chocolate on her breath.

"I have been unable to find my glass case today," the woman stated. She gestured with her hands to indicate the size of the case. "It's about this big. Dark blue. I've been looking for it all morning, but can't seem to find it anywhere. Do you think?"

"Think what?" Bess asked.

"I was just thinking that perhaps it was stolen, too," the woman mumbled, her eyes widening after her statement.

"I doubt it," Bess said without hesitation. "A wallet is a valuable thing. A glass case, while of value to the owner, may not be of much value to someone else."

"I see," the woman softly replied, casting her eyes to the floor.

Suddenly, Bess felt like one of those nurses. The kind that dismisses every problem, every question, every concern with a wave of the hand and an attribution to old age. Bess looked at the woman and smiled.

"If I find the guilty party," she said. "I will be certain to ask about your glass case."

Bess cupped her hands in a size that was similar to the size of the woman's hands.

"This big?" she asked.

"That's correct," the woman answered with a smile. "Thank you."

Bess showed herself out the door. When she closed it, she pulled hard, but the door would not latch itself closed. She looked at the door, sitting ajar, and simply shook her head. Having the door to her room always open was not something Bess would enjoy.

As she walked down the hallway to continue her questioning, Bess noticed that the doors to each of the rooms were also not quite closed all the way. She was careful to knock on each door so as not to push them open the way she did with the first room she visited. Each person she spoke with did not remember hearing or seeing anything the previous night. In addition to not seeing or hearing anything, Bess discovered one more thing that all the rooms had in common. Every person had lost or misplaced something of value over the last few days. They were small things. A scarf. A stuffed animal. A tissue box. When they pointed to where the items were left, Bess noted that they were all left on low tables or shelves close to the door. Nothing had been taken from a closet, a drawer, or a high table.

As she walked back to her room, Bess began to wonder about two things. She knew why someone would take a wallet, but a tissue box or glass case didn't make sense. Also, why in this hallway? Why would someone take things from just these rooms and not any other ones? Indeed, there was something strange going on in this particular hallway. How would she know for sure who was stealing these things?

CURIOSITY OVER CARDS

It was a Tuesday morning. For Bess, Tuesday mornings meant getting her mind active with a rousing game of bridge. She found her friends in the Game Room, where she always found them on a Tuesday. Helen Gruber, Flo Morgenstern, and Rose Grumbine were all seated at a round table, making small talk when Bess finally arrived.

"Ruth Moore is turning one hundred soon," she heard Rose say.

"It's been a while since we've had someone turn a hundred here at Honey Hills," Helen observed.

"Do you think the newspapers will come?" Flo asked.

"All I know is they're planning a party for her," Rose replied.

Silence filled the next few minutes as Bess sat down. Flo handed her a deck of cards and asked Bess to deal. While she shuffled the cards, Bess took note of everyone's eyes on her in anticipation of what cards would be dealt to whom. With all the attention on her, Bess thought this would be a good time to make an announcement.

"Someone is stealing things from Chet Wooden's room," Bess stated.

When she finished saying those words, she began to deal the cards. After the last card was dealt, Bess looked up at the faces of her friends. Rose and Helen both took a few seconds to look at Bess before their eyes returned to their cards. Flo Morgenstern kept her eyes locked on her cards, causing Bess to think she must have been holding a good hand.

"So what was stolen?" Helen finally asked.

"He seems to be missing his wallet," Bess replied, playing her first card.

"Probably just misplaced it," Helen mumbled.

Silence followed as each person laid out a flurry of cards on the table. Then there was a pause as Flo considered what card to play next.

"I heard that the air conditioning isn't working in Chet's hallway," Helen announced while she closely examined her cards. "I heard one of the maintenance men say they were having trouble with the humidity in that hallway. He said they couldn't even get the doors to the rooms closed because the wood doors have swelled up so much. Can you imagine trying to sleep with all the hot weather we've been having?"

"So have you told someone about this...thief?" Rose Grumbine finally asked for the first time, turning her eyes to Bess.

"No," Bess answered. "First, I will try to find the person responsible."

Again, she could sense that her words were met with an uneasy silence. Now even Flo had placed her good hand of cards down on the table and was looking directly at Bess. Rose and Helen also joined in the group stare.

"You shouldn't put yourself in such a position, Bess," Rose said, lowering her cards. "It might not be a safe thing to do. Tell someone in security. Let them take care of it. I'll call security as soon as I get back to my room if you'd like. That's their job you know."

"Ladies," Bess said, putting her cards down and clearing her throat. "I may soon be eighty years old. I may have lost my Marilyn Monroe looks years ago. I may not be able to swim twenty laps in the public pool the way I used to. Age has stripped me of many things, but I still have a first class mind in a world where there seems to be more second class thinkers. It is my experience with law enforcement that people who usually commit petty crimes are second class thinkers. They don't think things through and they certainly don't think about consequences. As I said, I may not have my looks and I may not have my muscles but my mind will allow me to outthink whoever is committing these thefts."

Bess let out a sigh when she couldn't think of anything more to say. Flo, Helen, and Rose all had their cards down on the table. They were all smiling and they were all looking right at Bess.

"I think you should do it," Rose finally said.

"So do I," Helen added.

"Me too," Flo said, adjusting her glasses. "Like you said, just because we all live here doesn't mean we have to stop using the skills we know best. It doesn't mean we have to stop doing things we're good at."

"So how do you plan on catching this thief?" Rose asked.

"I have an idea," Bess replied. "I need to run it by Chet, but I think it will work."

For the next few minutes, Bess shared her plan with her friends. The more she spoke, the more confident she felt that what she was planning would actually work. The quiet nods and words of encouragement from her friends merely reinforced her idea for catching this thief. Thanks to the company of her friends, she now felt more prepared to talk to Chet about her plan for recovering his wallet.

CRIME AND CONFLICT

"You want to do what?" Chet asked.

"You heard me," Bess replied. "It's the only way I can think of to discover whose been coming into the rooms in your hallway."

"You want us to switch rooms?" Chet asked.

"Just for a night, maybe two," Bess suggested.

She watched Chet's face react to this idea. While he appeared to be able to adapt and adjust to most any step on the dance floor, the suggestion of him sleeping in another bed for a few nights seemed to throw Chet off balance. She could see it in how his eye brows lowered and how he seemed to chew on something in his mouth, even though she knew his mouth was empty. She could also see it in how his eyes turned away from her and down to the floor.

"What would people think?" Chet finally asked. He looked at Bess and his eyebrows slowly rose. "What if someone saw you going into my room at night in your robe? Or worse, what if they see you come out in the morning? What would people have to say about that?"

"I'm quite certain that people may say the same thing when they see a gentleman going into my room late at night and not emerging," Bess replied. "If anyone has a question about it, I'll set them straight. Wouldn't you want do the same thing?"

Chet grew silent for a moment. He stopped chewing, locked his jaw and gave Bess a firm nod of his head.

"If there is someone stealing things," Chet remarked, "we must make sacrifices to find out who they are. Let people say whatever they want about me. My honor isn't as important as righting a wrong."

Chet's words caused Bess to take a deep breath. It seemed that Chet was merely concerned about his honor, but *her* honor never graced his lips. As was so often the case in life, Bess thought, having one perspective on someone was so much easier than seeing people in more than one light. She knew Chet from dancing. He had been a perfect gentleman on the mornings they danced for a few hours. He had been a perfect gentleman on those moments when they'd pass or see each other around the hallways of the Honey Hills Retirement Home. That was the Chet that caused her heart to stir. The fearful, self-conscious, self-centered man before her now was not the gentleman she had felt so strongly for. The revelation caused her to take another sigh, then smile and nod at Chet.

"We will find your wallet," she said in a clear tone

For the next few nights, well after the nurses were done with their rounds, Bess found herself putting her idea to the test by swapping rooms with Chet. The first night caused her some adjustments to sleeping in a new room. First, she found his bed to be rather large for her small frame. She also found the room's décor a bit more tailored to a man's tastes than a woman's. There were plenty of references to his days as a hunter. Pictures of him with friends standing over deer and even a black bear that she guessed he shot. The photos caused her to wonder how someone who could be so graceful on the dance floor could go out and kill an animal. Hunting was a sport that she just didn't understand. She used to carry a gun as a police officer and was happy that she never had to use it.

Another thing her eyes lingered on in Chet's room were the photos of him and his wife. His wife sat in the picture frame, with Chet's arm around her, smiling out at Bess while she lay in Chet's bed at night. The expression on her face caused Bess to feel a little guilty for even thinking that she had feelings for him. One night, she decided it would make her feel better if she addressed the picture.

"He's a very nice man," Bess said to the photo. "You were very lucky to have such a gentleman for a husband. I won't be asking him for anything more than a dance once a week. That is a promise from one lady to another."

The words made Bess feel better. That night, when she turned out the light, she lay on his bed thinking about *her* husband, and how *he* would have felt seeing her dance with another man. He probably would have smiled and waved her on, happy to know that he would not be subjected to such an activity.

As she prepared to drift off to sleep, thinking about dancing and Chet and her husband, Bess began to notice a narrow beam of light that appeared on the floor in front of the bed. It was a sliver of light coming from the hallway. She slipped on her glasses and watched as the narrow light slowly grew wider.

Bess remained perfectly still, afraid to move too quickly to scare off whoever was walking into the room. Her mind was racing and she was curious to see who it was who was entering. Her eyes lingered on the clock, noting it was well past midnight. Once inside, she listened to how quiet the intruder was moving around the room. She could hear the intruder breathing right next to her bed. Finally, she sat up and turned her head in one full motion to get a better view of who was in the room. She turned on a light and was surprised at what she found.

"Bart?" Bess whispered to herself.

There standing in the room, with his nose sniffing and dripping, was Bart the therapy dog. Bart was a large friendly Golden Retriever whose only purpose in life, Bess thought, was to wag his tail and let people pet him. It was a good rapport Bart had with the residents of the Honey Hills Retirement Home. Most days, Bart would be led around the center on a leash by a nurse. Wherever he went, Bart usually brought out smiles in residents who didn't smile all that much. In return for the smiles he caused, Bart got plenty of belly rubs, not to mention free meals and a place to sleep. However, it appeared that Bart was not sleeping much tonight.

She remained in bed watching him sniff and burry his nose into a coat that Chet had left on a chair. Bart stepped back, his long narrow head slowly moving from side to side. Next, he made his way over to Chet's closet. He pawed at the closet door, causing the door to pop open. Bess then watched as Bart dipped his head down into the shadows, stepped back from the closet, and quietly made his way out the door and into the hallway.

"Oh, dear," Bess said, quickly getting out of bed and trying to keep her balance. She was never that good at getting up fast from bed, and the fact that she was in the dark made it a bit more challenging. She stood perfectly still for a moment, the sound of both knees cracking beneath her, then quickly stepped towards the door. When she stepped out of her room, she spotted Bart strolling up the hallway, his tail wagging while he walked. Bess turned and quickly followed Bart up the hall.

She pursued Bart around a corner, getting close but not too close to cause Bart to start running. Then she saw Bart stop in front of a door. He pawed at the door once, then pushed it open with his nose and slipped inside. Bess quickly made her way to the door. She didn't see a name on the door, so she knew there wasn't a resident inside. Rather than knocking, Bess placed her hand on the door and gave it a good push. Like all the other doors in the hallway, this one was also swelled from the humidity and not quite closed. Bess simply pushed the door open. There on the floor of the empty room, amidst a pile of towels and sheets, Bess found Bart lying with Chet's black slipper in his mouth. Bart seemed to sense that Bess did not approve of his actions.

"Put that down!" Bess said with a wave of her finger. "Bad dog, Bart! Bad dog!"

Bart let out a low moan as he dropped the slipper from his mouth. He dipped his head down, nestled his chin between his paws, and looked up at Bess with his large brown eyes.

"Oh, Bart," Bess said, feeling her anger subside when she looked at his big brown eyes.

She knelt down and began to feel around the floor. There under some of the bed sheets scattered around the ground she found a blue glass case. She also found a bar of soap. She felt around some more and located someone's hair brush.

"My goodness, Bart, you have been busy," Bess said.

Bart merely stared at her, then shifted his head from between his paws to beside his paws and let out another moan. Slowly, Bart rolled over on his side and in a matter of seconds began to fall asleep on one of the sheets. While she watched him close his eyes, Bess continued to feel around and under the pile of sheets and the towels. Then her hand came across something rather large, round, and what felt like leather. Out from under a pile of white sheets, she pulled up a wallet that fit the description Chet had given her. She looked inside, and pulled out a card with his name on it just to be sure. Bess stood up, her hands filled with a variety of things and surveyed the scene of towels and sheets.

"You've made quite a mess here, Bart," Bess sighed. "I'm afraid this bit of shenanigans is going to have to stop."

In a matter of minutes, Bess was able to locate one of the few nurses working overnight and showed her the room where Bart had fallen asleep amidst the towels and sheets. Bess also showed the nurse the collection of items Bart had stolen from the rooms in the hallway.

"Oh my gosh," was all the nurse could say over and over again. "I just let Bart out when I knew everyone was asleep and their doors were closed. Most nights he'd just lay in the hallway. I thought it would be good security to have a dog out and about. Besides, he's good company for me. I never thought...oh my gosh."

Bess cleared her throat and took a step closer to the nurse.

"I understand," Bess said. "Perhaps Bart should have a more secure place to sleep in at night. A place that would keep him out of trouble. Would you agree?"

"Well of course," the nurse nodded. She turned to Bess and let out a sigh. "Please don't tell anyone about this. I've only been here a few weeks and I like working here."

Bess could quickly recognize the worry on the nurse's face. She appeared to be one of the younger nurses, new to the job and getting stuck working overnight shifts because of her lack of experience at the Honey Hills. Bess smiled and tried to relieve some of the nurse's tension.

"It will be okay," Bess replied, raising her hand. "You're heart was in the right place. How were you to know what a curious dog would do in a hallway filled with doors that don't close? As I said, a secure place for Bart would be a safer place for him."

"You're right," the nurse replied. It was one of the few times that she heard any nurse say that to her since moving into Honey Hills. The words caused Bess to smile. It was a smile of pride in being told that she was right by a nurse. For as Bess had learned since moving to Honey Hills, the nurses were *always* right.

The next morning, she spotted Chet in the hallway walking in his robe and slippers. It wasn't unusual for some residents to be out in their pajamas or robe in the morning. Some liked to grab a cup of coffee. Other's liked to get a morning paper and take it back to their room to read. Bess didn't feel out of place in her robe as she walked down the halls. Chet, she could tell, was clearly not as comfortable. Wearing a dark blue robe, matching slippers, and his white hair neatly combed to the side, Chet looked as if he'd been up for hours. When they made eye contact, Chet quickly intercepted her in the hallway.

"Here," Bess said, holding up his wallet.

"You found it!" Chet beamed, a smile replacing the grim expression on his face. "Who took it?"

"Let's just say it was a misunderstanding," Bess grinned, choosing to keep Bart's identity a secret. "I've spoken to the culprit and he's promised to keep all four of his feet out of your room."

"All four feet?" Chet asked with a laugh at the end of his sentence.

"Like I said," Bess continued. "A misunderstanding that won't happen again."

Chet beamed as he cracked open his wallet. He glanced at the contents in an informal check of important things. When he finished he closed the wallet and slipped it into the pocket of his robe.

"Where did you learn how to do something like this?" Chet asked.

"Like what?" Bess asked.

"Solving crimes," Chet said. "Where did you learn to do that?"

"My father was a police detective," Bess explained. "Since he didn't have a son, he taught me everything he knew about how to investigate and solve mysteries."

"What did he teach you?" Chet asked.

"He taught me how to investigate people and not just the crime," Bess stated. "How it was important to really understand people and to have a gut feeling about them."

"Does that include four-footed people?" Chet laughed.

"No," Bess replied with a smile. "I just had a feeling about the people here at the Honey Hills Retirement Home. It didn't seem possible to me that someone would intentionally be going into rooms and stealing things. A theft is usually a crime committed for reasons involving money. Everyone here is so well provided for, with meals and shelter, money isn't a necessity for people here at Honey Hills. That was the question at hand for me. That was the mystery."

"I see," Chet sighed. He adjusted the sash on his robe. "Well, I appreciate what you've done, Bess. Thank you."

She could see his eyes were only half open. She also noted how his hands hung from the pockets of his robe. If she hadn't known better, Bess would have guessed that Chet hadn't slept at all.

"You seem tired," Bess observed. "Was my bed not comfortable enough for you?"

"I just couldn't bring myself to sleep in your room," Chet explained. "I walked around for part of the first night, then found a comfortable chair to sleep on in the north wing of the building. That's where I've been sleeping the last couple of nights. It's actually a nice and quiet spot."

"Well," Bess said, a bit surprised by the news. She shook her head and her mouth hung open while she looked at him. One question hung in the air. She took a deep breath and finally asked what words were lingering behind her lips. "Why didn't you sleep in my room?"

"I told you before," Chet answered in a soft tone. "I

have a reputation to think of. I can't be seen coming out of your bedroom. What would people think of me?"

"I came out of *your* bedroom!" Bess stated in a louder tone of voice. "Are you more worried about what people will think of me or you?"

Chet opened his mouth to reply but nothing came out. The question caught him off guard, Bess thought. The lack of any kind of response was causing her blood pressure to go up with each passing second. She could feel herself getting hotter the longer he looked at her in a lingering quiet stare. Finally, Bess turned and walked away, leaving Chet alone and in silence.

WAITING FOR ILLUMINATION

In the mornings, when the summer air was comfortable for the only time of the day, Bess enjoyed going out and sitting on the bench in front of the main entrance to the Honey Hills Retirement Home. The view from the bench was splendid; a full green field that stretched down a sloping hill to a quiet country road. On occasion, an Amish horse and buggy would pass. Bess enjoyed the sound the horse's hooves made on the road. She likened it to someone clapping two wooden blocks together. In the distance, a small farm sat in the middle of a large green pasture. Just beyond the farm, the sun hid behind the faint blue silhouette of mountains that stretched along the edge of the valley. Most mornings, Bess would watch as the sun slowly rose above the mountains and spilled into the field with light and color.

While the view was breathtaking, Bess equally enjoyed watching the nurses come and go from the Honey Hills Retirement Home. The first thing she'd notice was their walk. The younger nurses tended to have a hurried pace while the older nurses took more leisurely strides. Next Bess looked at their faces. Most nurses were looking down or staring straight ahead. No doubt, Bess thought, they were faces that were envisioning the tasks about to be undertaken. For nurses, that usually meant preparing medicine, waking patients, and reviewing logs from the previous night.

There was a lot to be learned by watching someone, Bess thought. While she hadn't worked as a police officer for a long time, her instincts for people never seemed to retire. Most days she was able to suppress her instincts. Keep them in check. She tried to pleasantly occupy her time with such everyday matters as television, puzzles, and books. They were more pleasant activities to engage her mind with, as opposed to thefts, crimes, and suspects. Yet, it was one thing to make a conscious choice to fill one's mind with pleasant thoughts and quite another to do pleasant things.

One cannot turn off instinct, Bess was beginning to realize. It wasn't like a car or a radio. Her instincts were almost like people. Sometimes she could hear her instincts' voices in her head and she couldn't just turn them off or ignore them. She was reminded of this when she sat on the bench and looked out at the various faces of nurses and visitors who came and went from the Honey Hills Retirement Home. On occasion, she would see a face that just didn't look quite right. Perhaps she'd see something in their eyes. Perhaps it was an expression on a face. Perhaps the clothes they wore. Bess couldn't quite put her finger on it, but she knew there was something about a person that caused her collective instincts to rise up and say with a clear voice that only Bess could hear, "Watch that one."

This morning, Bess was pleasantly surprised to see her daughter, Samantha, walking up the sidewalk leading to the bench. What made Bess smile even more was seeing her grand-daughter, Nicole, skipping behind her mother.

Nicole was soon going to turn four years of age. She had boundless energy that she usually channeled by skipping, swinging her arms, tapping her feet, or simply looking around to catch a glimpse of any slight movement she detected. Bess couldn't help but to smile at Nicole's keen sense for observation. Nothing happened without her knowing it, which Bess thought made Nicole a chip off the old block.

Samantha, however, did not inherit her mother's instincts for people. This was never more evident than when she chose to marry a man that Bess could clearly see was not a good choice. She told Samantha this on more than one occasion, but Samantha insisted on following her heart. Years later, Samantha and her husband were now getting a divorce.

"Well this is a pleasant surprise," Bess grinned at her two girls.

"Mother," Samantha scolded. "The air is cool out here. You should have your sweater."

"Nonsense," Bess said with a wave of her hand. "The fresh air feels good. Besides, it'll be hot in another hour. I sit out here every morning and I know that sun is going to get *very* hot by breakfast time."

"Morning, Nana," Nicole chirped while standing on one foot and holding her arms out on either side. "Look, I can dance like a ballerina."

"So you can," Bess said, reaching out and wrapping her arms around Nicole. She could hear Nicole giggle as she gave her a hug. When Bess looked up, she could see Samantha standing, hands on hips, drumming her fingers with nervous energy.

"Mom," Samantha said, stepping up behind Nicole and placing her hand on Nicole's curly brown hair. "I stopped by to tell you I contacted the bank. I told them we were no longer interested in closing your savings account."

"Thank you," Bess said, her eyes meeting Samantha's for the first time. The news caused Bess to feel a smile come across her face. Samantha's face remained without expression. It was the perfect opportunity, Bess thought, for both women to be happy. They had resolved an issue that was causing bitter feelings. An issue that had led Bess and Samantha to exchange hard words not so long ago. Yet, Samantha stood there unable to see all of this, Bess thought. There must be more, Bess reasoned.

"Go ahead, my dear," Bess said with a knowing nod. "I can tell something's on your mind. What is it?"

"I had my attorney draw up this paper," Samantha said, reaching into her purse and pulling out a business-sized envelope.

"Attorney?" Bess said, grabbing the envelope from Samantha's hand.

"It's a document that puts me in charge of your estate should anything happen to you," Samantha said, her eyes flicking to the side. "My attorney thought it would be a good idea and I agree."

"But nothing is wrong with me," Bess said, glancing at Nicole and smiling.

"I know, Mother," Samantha said, "but if something were to happen, like a stroke or a heart attack, and you couldn't act on your own then I'd be in charge of making your financial decisions for you."

The statement hung in the air without reply. Bess sat back in her bench and took a slow deep breath.

"Please sign the papers, mother," Samantha said, pulling a pen from her purse.

"I told you I'm fine," Bess said holding the paper up. "What is all this about?"

"It's about loose ends," Samantha said, her voice trailing off.

"What do you mean?" Bess asked.

"Mother, my life is a bundle of loose ends," Samantha sighed, sitting down. Bess watched as her eyes began to blink a little faster. "My divorce is still pending. I've got loose ends with my attorney and his fees. Loose ends with my ex about who's gonna get what and who isn't going to get what in the settlement. I've got loose ends at work. I've got loose ends every evening with Nicole trying to help her with school, her friends, and what clothes she likes and doesn't like. Then I have you, and the loose ends of your care and your estate."

Bess watched as Samantha pulled up her purse, dipped her hand inside, and pulled out her cell phone.

"You know why I carry this with me all the time?" Samantha asked. "The cell phone you always say I talk to more than you? I don't carry it around with me because it's fun. This cell phone *is* my life right now, mom. It keeps my head above water."

"So I'm a loose end?" Bess asked.

"Not you, mother," Samantha explained. "Just your matters. Like the bank. Like that paper your holding. All of the little things that you need to be taken care of just fall right into my lap."

"I see," Bess said. Her eyes turned to Nicole who was occupying herself by skipping up and down a set of steps.

"C'mon, Mother," Samantha said, getting up from the bench. "I'm your daughter for heaven's sakes. I'm your only child. I may be a bit bossy from time to time, but you are my mother. I'm going to take care of you."

"Let me read it," Bess said, putting the paper back in the envelope and holding it with both hands.

"Fine," Samantha sighed. She looked at her cell phone, bit her bottom lip, then looked around. She was always a bundle of nervous energy, Bess thought. Even as a young girl, Bess could recall how Samantha was always trying to catch a glimpse of everything that was going on around her. She would always be looking, listening, even smelling the things that surrounded her. In some ways, Bess could still see the child in her grown-up daughter.

"Well we need to get going," Samantha finally stated, glancing at her watch.

"Stay," Bess quickly said. She reached out and grabbed Samantha's hand. "I come out here every morning to enjoy this view. I like to watch how the sun slowly pulls over the mountain and lights up the colors in that field over there. In about ten minutes, the sun will fill that field.

Right now it looks dark, but soon you'll see bright green grass. You'll even be able to see some different colored flowers blooming in that field. I'm always amazed at how a little illumination can change how you see things."

Her words caused Samantha to stop and slowly sit down. While she kept her hand on Samantha's, she noticed that Samantha's fingers were not reaching, moving, or lacing them- selves around Bess's fingers. With Nicole doing a perfect pirouette in front of them, Bess and Samantha sat quietly, stared into the shadows and waited for the illumination to begin.

STILL A MOTHER

Bess carried the envelope with her for most of the day. She carried it to lunch. She carried it to Bridge Club. She tossed it on the table for her lady friends to see and then frowned at it as if it were some foul smelling animal she found in the street.

"My daughter gave me this," Bess stated, pointing at the envelope.

"Is it a card?" Flo Morgenstern asked.

"Is it your birthday?" Helen Gruber asked, nervously adjusting her few strands of hair.

"No," Bess quietly answered, picking up the cards dealt to her. "It seems I'm a loose end for my daughter. Something to be dealt with…like a shoe lace. Something to be secured so she doesn't have to be bothered with me."

"What are you talking about?" Rose Grumbine asked, resting her elbows on the table.

"There are papers in this envelope that my daughter's lawyer wants me to sign," Bess explained, pointing to the envelope. "Seems that if anything happens to me then my daughter gets control of my life."

"Oh my gosh!" Flo laughed. "Look where you're sitting. You're living here *because* of your daughter, Bess. Our children already have control over us. Isn't that why we're all here?"

"No," Bess quickly responded, pointing a finger at Flo. "I am here because I wanted to come. My home and my grounds were too much work for me. When my husband died, I made a go of it for a year, then decided that coming here wasn't such a bad idea. It wasn't *her* choice it was mine."

"I signed one of those," Rose spoke up, her eyes locking on the envelope. "It wasn't a big deal to me. I know my kids will take care of me no matter what."

Bess sat quietly after Rose's statement. Her eyes moved from side to side across the table top. She reached out and tapped the envelope with her hand. She looked at Rose and realized that what she said had created a small window through which Bess could now understand why she felt the way she did. Why she felt so much anger.

"I don't trust my daughter," Bess quietly stated. She looked at the faces of her closest friends around her and felt as though she had uttered a bad word. She cleared her throat. "Is that a terrible thing to say? I mean, shouldn't a mother be able to trust her daughter?"

"Ideally," Helen Gruber spoke up. "I have three of them, Bess. You have one. My girls can make me three times as happy or three times as sad. I love my daughters but we still have our differences."

Bess grew silent. She picked up the cards from the table in front of her, slid the envelope back on her lap, and looked around at her friends.

"Let's play cards," Bess said with a smile.

For the rest of the day, Bess walked around the air conditioned hallways, glancing out windows at the steamy afternoon that filled the summer day. She caught a glimpse of people in shorts and T-shirts walking around the grounds from nearby neighborhoods. She watched one man, an employee at Honey Hills, cutting the grass. She noted the sweat that he wore on his forehead and that occasionally dripped from his brow. She also walked to another hallway where she had a clear view of the Honey Hills Retirement Home's daycare facility. She watched the young children outside running and playing. Their faces were pink. Their hair shined with a dewy sweat. Yet, their legs still managed to move very quickly.

It was during this point in her walk that Bess began to think about trust. When they dated, she was quite uncertain about getting married to her husband. Twice her husband got down on one knee, under an old oak tree where they first met at a country fair, and proposed to her. The first time he did so, she cried and whispered "no." The response led to some awkward moments and conversation. What it came down to, she recalled, was that she had trouble trusting the people she loved. She begged him for more time, he agreed, and they dated for two more years. When he brought her back to the same tree, got down on one knee in the same spot, and asked her to marry him again she quickly said yes.

Trust was not something that came easily to Bess. When she was a mother, her relationship with her daughter meant that Samantha was the one who had to do all the trusting. It was Samantha who had to trust that Bess would pick her up at the bus stop. Samantha had to trust that Bess would provide her with good meals and clean clothes. Samantha had to trust that Bess would always love her no matter what mistakes she made growing up.

Life had a way of turning the tables on Bess. Now that Samantha was grown, and Bess was much older, it was Bess who found herself having to trust Samantha. In some respects, the revelation made Bess feel like that young girl being proposed to again under that tall oak tree. After an afternoon of reflection, Bess decided that time would be the only way she would learn to accept what Samantha had asked her to sign. Time would be the only way she would learn to trust that her daughter could take care of her. At the age of eighty, Bess was quite confident that she would have a good amount of time to let that trust grow.

Later in the day, after her dinner, Bess heard a knock on her door. When she opened the door she found her neighbor, Charlotte, standing in front of her holding baby Jonah. There was something in Charlotte's eyes, an expression of both worry and concern, which Bess quickly recognized.

"Charlotte?" Bess asked. "Is everything okay?"

"I just got sick in the bathroom," Charlotte whispered, slumping against the door.

"Oh dear," Bess sighed. "Are you alright?"

"My stomach is sore," Charlotte moaned. "I'm afraid I'm coming down with something. Whatever it is I don't want Jonah to catch it. Would you...I mean...could you keep Jonah for a few hours until my daughter comes for him?"

"Of course," Bess said, quickly taking Jonah from Charlotte's arms. Bess was surprised at how easily Jonah made the switch. His eyes carefully shifted to Bess and a broad smile pushed up his full pink cheeks.

"Thank you," Charlotte said, slightly hunched over. "My daughter should be by for him around eight this evening. I'll put a note on my door so she'll know to come here."

"That's fine," Bess said, finding herself getting quite enamored with Jonah's blue eyes and his sweet smell. "Are we going to play? Are we going to play in my room?"

Jonah fussed and began to kick his chubby legs and small feet.

"Here," Charlotte said, ducking into her room and pulling out a stroller. "He likes when I push him around the hallways in this. Sometimes he even falls asleep."

Bess placed Jonah in the stroller. The kicking legs quickly stopped once he was inside. Bess looked at Charlotte, clutching her stomach with her eyes closed.

"We'll be just fine," Bess said with a nod to Charlotte. "You'd best get back inside and lay down."

With those last words, Charlotte quietly returned to her room. Bess looked down at Jonah and began to push the stroller. She glanced at Jonah from time to time and smiled at his head of blond hair moving from side to side. On occasion, his head would remain still, as if focused on something that they were passing. When she saw him point, Bess would slow down the stroller and let him look at a painting, or a flower, or whatever it was that engaged him.

As she walked, Bess began to feel those motherly emotions bubble again. The same feelings she had when she held Jonah for the first time. Those long dormant instincts and emotions that came with being a mother were being ignited. It was almost like this little child was running around inside of her heart, switching on lights in places that had long been dark.

Another thing Bess observed were the faces of the residents as they walked by and saw Bess pushing the stroller. There were more women than men at the Honey Hills Retirement Home. That wasn't just true here, that seemed to be a general rule in life. For whatever reason, husbands always seemed to pass on before their wives. There were many theories for this. Bess always thought that since women were the bringers of life into this world, God must bless them with a little extra time. When she looked at the smiles and the laughter of the women who walked by Jonah, she thought about the irony of the situation.

The Honey Hills Retireent Home was a place filled with women, most of whom had the privilege of being mothers. They had babies. They carried babies around, changed diapers, fed them, played with them, and loved them. Like Bess, other mothers also had those skills and those feelings laid to rest when their children got older.

Yet, all it took was one little child, like Jonah, to remind these women that no matter what their age, no matter what their ailment, they were always first and foremost mothers. Having a baby like Jonah at the Honey Hills Retirement Home simply reinforced that belief not just for Bess, but for every mother they passed on their long walk. When Jonah and Bess returned to her room, they found Charlotte's daughter waiting in front of her mother's room. She smiled and her long blond hair spilled over her shoulders when she stepped towards Bess. Jonah was clearly happy to see his mother and squealed when she scooped him up.

"Thank you," Jonah's mother said in a soft voice.

"No, thank you," Bess said with a smile.

As she watched Jonah wiggle in his mother's arms, Bess couldn't help but think about all the women who saw Jonah this evening. All the older women who, for a few seconds, were reminded that beneath their many wrinkles, white hair and glasses, they were still and would always be mothers.

CHICKEN TROUBLE

Days flew by and before Bess knew it, Tuesday morning had arrived and she found herself in her most favorite position of the week. She found herself seated at a table in the Honey Hills Recreation Room. She was seated at a table engaged in cards and conversations with her friends. At the moment, the focus of all four ladies was on their cards. The silence that added to the tension of this particular hand was broken when Rose Grumbine announced,

"I see that our chicken friend is back in town." Rose's words were followed by a knowing glance which she cast in the direction of Flo Morgenstern. "You remember him?"

"Does he still have that corn cob pipe hanging out of his mouth?" Flo asked, her eye brows going up at the end of her question.

"Yes," Rose laughed. "Filthy habit even for a chicken, don't you agree?"

"Quite," Flo nodded with a smile. "And those bright red pants. What on earth does a chicken need with bright red pants anyway?"

Both ladies finished their comments, smiled, and turned their eyes to Bess. The idea of having others knowingly keep a secret was always a pet peeve for Bess. It was a quality she could never shake from her school girl days. She always had a driving desire to know things, especially secret things. She allowed the silence to build for a few more seconds until she could no longer resist indulging in that school girl habit.

"Would one of you please tell me what on Earth you're talking about," Bess finally spoke up.

"Every summer three things come to the Honey Hills Retirement Home," Rose explained. "First comes the hot and humid weather, then the beautiful flowers, and finally a pipe smoking chicken with bright red pants."

"Yes," Helen Gruber laughed. "He's not the most welcomed visitor at Honey Hills but he seems to keep coming back year after year. Oh, and did she mention that he's ten feet tall?"

"A chicken can't be that big," Bess said with a wave of her hand. She pointed her finger at Helen, Rose and Flo. "You three keep talking like that and the nurses are going to be switching your medication doses."

"We're telling the truth," Rose said, lowering her cards. She pointed across the table at Bess. "You need to go outside and walk by the parking lot some morning. I know you like to take your morning walks around the back of the Honey Hills grounds from time to time, but you need to take a walk around the front parking lot. That's where you'll find that pipe chomping, red pants wearing chicken we've been talking about."

"Why would the Honey Hills Retirement Home agree to let something like that here?" Bess asked.

"It's here to promote the Home's Summer Barbeque?" Rose explained. "They put the chicken up early in the summer to gain attention and interest for the event."

"Tackiest thing I've ever seen," Helen chimed in. "Every year they blow that thing up and tie it by the side of the road. All this work for some precious fundraiser."

"So why do they need a fundraiser?" Bess asked.

"It's a fundraiser for the Honey Hills Retirement Home," Rose answered.

"With all we're paying," Bess stated, looking around the table, "they shouldn't have to raise money for this place."

"Actually," Rose began, "there are various groups that go bowling, take bus trips, and do other things that require some money. This is a fundraiser for those groups. It's not necessarily for Honey Hills, but for its residents."

"I see," Bess nodded. "So that's why that rooster..."

"Chicken," Flo interrupted, glancing over her glasses at Bess. "That's why that chicken with bright red pants and a corn cob pipe is standing in front of the entrance to our retirement community."

"Yes," Rose nodded. "He's standing right next to the sign that reads, 'Honey Hills: Retirement with Dignity.'"

"Dignity," Flo huffed and she tapped her cards on the table top. "There's nothing dignified about a ten foot tall chicken with a corn cob pipe hanging out of his mouth."

"My husband used to smoke a pipe," Helen smiled. "I thought it made him look rather dignified. You know Bing Crosby used to smoke a pipe?"

"So what are we going to do about this?" Bess asked. Her eyes scanned the table and for the first time all morning. The ladies around her sat with little to say.

"About what?" Flo finally asked.

"It sounds like you all are up in arms about this chicken thing," Bess continued. She leaned in closer to her friends and spoke in a softer tone. "If there's one thing I learned about working as a police officer, it was how to help people solve their problems. I was amazed at how many creative solutions I could think of to keep people happy. So, do you want me to think of something to help with this problem?"

"I do," Rose quickly answered. She looked around the table and smiled. "Let me explain. I have relatives coming to visit me this weekend and they laughed at me over the phone when I told them to look for the building with the big chicken wearing red pants. I could hear this long pause over the phone and I could tell they thought I must have been loopy. So yes, I for one would be happy with a solution."

"Whatever your solution," Flo began, "I'm afraid we won't be much help. Rose has arthritis. I have bursitis in my shoulder. It's not like we can pick that fellow up and carry him away."

"I know," Bess responded. "It seems to me that there is a third solution out there just waiting to be found. We don't need to live with this indignity, ladies, but we don't need to do something drastic like kidnap our feathered friend. It seems to me there should be another way, but I just haven't thought of it yet."

"Well, that barbeque isn't for another two months," Rose explained. "I for one don't care to spend another summer staring at a chicken in the front parking lot."

All eyes turned to Bess and the expressions on their faces told her that they were hoping she would find a way to rid them of their problem.

For the rest of the day, Bess thought about the chicken predicament. She thought about it all through dinner. She thought about it while she ate her slice of apple pie for dessert. She remained at her dinner table long after all the other ladies were gone to think about it some more. She remained seated, scooping up small pieces of her pie onto her fork and slowly chewing each bite while she debated solutions. Occasionally, she even mumbled to herself between bites.

"How does one get rid of a ten foot tall chicken?" Bess quietly asked herself. She thought about the ridiculous nature of the question, laughed to herself, then looked around to see if anyone had heard her question.

In the evening she pondered her question a bit more while she wandered the hallways, staring down at the blue rug under her feet. She stopped in front of one window where she gazed out at the garden. It was usually in the evening that she saw a maintenance worker come and bring a hose to water the plants in this particular garden. Bess loved to garden and she kept a watchful eye over this small garden in the center's courtyard. Sometimes her intense feelings for the flowers and their care made her more of a mother, checking on the garden a few times a week. After a while, she checked her watch and noticed that the maintenance man was indeed running late. The sun had dipped low in the sky and an egg-shaped moon was becoming more distinct by the minute. Having grown more concerned about the flowers being watered, Bess walked up to a nurse's station and inquired about the wayward maintenance man. Bess thought that a day as hot as this one would surely warrant some watering of a garden, even a small garden like this one.

"I don't really know where he is," the nurse replied with a shrug. Bess watched the nurse turn and speak with an older nurse seated at a desk behind her. She watched both nurses point towards the window and nod. The older nurse looked up at Bess and cleared her throat.

"I heard on the news we're gonna get some bad thunderstorms late morning tomorrow," the older nurse explained. "Maybe they decided not to water tonight and wait for those storms."

"I see," Bess nodded and walked away.

With that bit of news, Bess wandered back to her room. She turned on the TV and began to think about the fact that this summer had been a dry one. If what the nurse said was true, they would be getting rain for the first time in weeks. It would be rain that was desperately needed by all the gardens around Honey Hills's grounds. She flipped on the TV in time to see a weather report describing the coming day's forecast.

"Better tie down anything on your porch tomorrow morning," the weather man grinned at Bess from the TV screen. "There's gonna be a fast moving storm system passing through here late tomorrow morning. Since it's gonna be a fast moving system, we should get plenty of high winds along with some rain. You'll have plenty of sticks and branches to pick up tomorrow afternoon when this storm is done."

Bess smiled. Suddenly she knew what she would be doing early tomorrow morning. First she would pay a visit to Helen Gruber. Helen, like Bess, was also a gardening enthusiast. Unlike Bess, Helen managed to keep a set of gardening tools in her room even though she didn't have a garden to tend with them. Bess wasn't interested in working in a garden tomorrow, but there was something productive she thought of doing with Helen's tools. Something that involved a chicken.

TROWELING FOR A CHICKEN

Early the next morning, Bess strolled out the front doors of the Honey Hills Retirement Home. Bright sunshine caused her to squint and the hot air seemed to smother her the second she set foot out of the Honey Hills' cool confines. However, her eyes locked onto something that lingered just beyond the cars that packed the parking lot. Bess made her way through the parking lot and then stopped by the side of the road that ran in front of the Honey Hills Retirement Home. Next to the road, anchored in the grass by two thick ropes, she found the much discussed chicken.

It was very tall, rivaling a nearby tree in height. It had a large white belly that curved into a bright red pair of pants. The chicken also had bright red suspenders that attached to the pants and ran over the chicken's shoulders. She could also see something running out of the chicken's mouth and guessed it was the pipe.

"Aren't you quite the spectacle," Bess mumbled over her glasses at the tall bird. She walked around him wondering how something that was twice her size could be removed from the premises by someone of her slight build and height. She ran her hand along one of the ropes that kept the chicken up right. She noted how each rope was attached to a wooden stake that was buried in the ground.

As she walked, Bess heard a low humming sound coming from the bird. She looked down while she walked and behind the chicken she found a small metal fan attached to the bottom of the bird. The fan was blowing and keeping the bird upright. Bess stepped close to see that the fan was blowing air in through an opening in the bird's tail feathers. The fan was actually secured to the latex of the chicken. Bess stepped back, looked at the chicken and smiled.

"I'm afraid I'm going to have to do something about you," she stated.

The bird smiled and stared off into the distance, as if trying to remain aloof and above such comments from something as small as Bess. She glanced down at the wooden stakes once more before turning and going back into the Honey Hills Retirement Home.

A few minutes later, she found herself standing in the room of Helen Gruber. Her entrance was greeted with a smile from Helen and her request for the tools to deal with the chicken problem was met with some surprise.

"You're really going to do this?" Helen asked.

Bess stood calmly in Helen's room, hands folded in front of her, an easy smile on her face.

"As I said," Bess replied, "I need to borrow your gardening tools so I can take care of that chicken problem."

"So you thought of a solution?" Helen grinned.

"I have," Bess replied.

"Are you going to pop it like a balloon?" Helen asked while she opened a closet door. She pulled out a white canvas bag with a red rose on it and placed it on her bed.

"Not necessarily," Bess laughed.

She watched as Helen slowly reached into her bag and pulled out each tool and laid it on the bed. Bess couldn't help but wonder how long it had been since Helen got them out to use.

"In the summer, I used to carry this bag out to my garden every day," Helen said with a wistful sigh. "Oh,

Bess, I can recall some days when I just left the bag in the garden because I knew I'd be out the next day. How I miss my garden."

"As do I, Helen," Bess said with a nod. "I used to spend all of my free time in my garden. It wasn't very big, but it was just enough for me."

Helen turned her eyes to the tools on the bed. She grabbed a small green shovel that still bore some dirt marks from past gardening adventures. She smiled at the tool and ran her fingers over the dirt marks as if they were scars of gardening days gone by. She looked at Bess and handed it to her.

"Did you want this trowel?" Helen asked, holding the small shovel up with her hand.

"That would be perfect," Bess answered.

"I have two trowels," Helen said, raising another one in the air. "Would you like some company for digging?"

"Of course I would enjoy the company of someone to kneel with and dig in the ground," Bess answered with a smile. "It would be fun to have someone to join me in weeding."

"Weeding?" Helen asked, her nose scrunching up. "That chicken isn't planted in a garden, Bess."

"I know," Bess answered, "but I think it could still use a little uprooting."

Together they ventured outside, Helen carrying her gardening bag and Bess carrying the trowel. They made their way over to where the chicken was fixed in the front yard of the Honey Hills Retirement Home. Bess stopped in front of the chicken. Helen stood next to her and she placed her bag down in the grass.

"Now what?" Helen asked, resting her hands on her hips.

"See those wooden stakes," Bess said, pointing at the ground on either side of the chicken. "Those are the only things holding this chicken to the ground. I want to use our trowels to dig up the ground around the stakes. Loosen those stakes up a bit."

"If we dig too much," Helen pointed out, "he'll just tip over and lay here in the yard. It won't take long for someone from maintenance to come out and put it right back in the ground."

"I don't want to make the stakes *that* loose," Bess responded. "I want to dig just enough so a good gust of wind will loosen our friend. You see, there are supposed to be some severe thunderstorms coming through here in a few hours. If our friend were to break loose during the storm, I'm thinking he'll get blown into one of the nearby farmer fields...maybe farther. Who knows how far he'll travel if this storm has enough wind to it."

"A storm won't blow something this big, Bess," Helen stated.

"Isn't it worth a try?" Bess asked.

The two ladies looked at each other, smiled, then slowly sat down on the grass. Helen pulled out her trowel which she proudly displayed in her hand for Bess to see. Together both ladies began to dig into the ground and excavate the soil around the wooden stakes. Because of a lack of rain, the ground was hard, causing Bess to grip her trowel a little tighter and push a little harder.

"Tell me why you wanted to do this?" Helen asked while she dug.

"You see, Helen, when I used to walk the streets of Venton as a police officer, I would meet two kinds of people," Bess explained. "There were those people who wanted things to change, but did nothing about it. They just kind of hoped things would get better all by themselves. What I found was that hoping things would get better didn't tend to make it so."

"And who were the second kind of people?" Helen asked.

"The second kind of people were those who wanted things to change and would do some-thing about it. They'd write letters, or hold meetings, or really take a lot of action to change their fortunes for the better. After a while, I began to realize I was one of those people who would use action to make things change. I guess that's why I brought you out here to help me…to change."

"Well that's fine with me," Helen answered. "I guess I'd rather do something and not be one of those people who just stands around hoping this chicken disappears."

Together both ladies continued to dig. Each had one stake to dig around. The ground was solid and Bess could feel her arthritis flare up in her hand. She winced and tried to keep her grip on the trowel. Then she smiled when the ground became looser and easier to dig. From time to time, Bess would glance over at Helen to see how she was doing. They both seemed to work at the same pace, loosening enough ground around the stake to where they could actually wiggle it with their hands. Bess finally reached down and rocked the wooden stake from side to side before standing up. It was truly quite loose, yet not loose enough that the chicken would drop to the ground. Bess walked over to where Helen was digging.

"Isn't it fun to get dirty again?" Helen asked with a laugh.

"Yes," Bess nodded. "I love getting down and smelling the grass. Smelling the soil. You're right, Helen, it is fun! It's also hard to stand up."

When they finished, they returned to Helen's room where they washed off the tools and each other's hands. They stood in the middle of the room for a few minutes, swapped stories about their gardens the way two adults would swap stories about their prized children. For some gardeners, Bess reasoned more than once, a garden was like a child. It required love, nurturing, and attention and in return it gave unconditional beauty.

After a few minutes of walking back to the front entrance, Bess found a seat in the vestibule to the main doors of the Honey Hills Retirement Home. It had been a good hour since she and Helen loosened the stakes around the chicken. In that one hour, the sky had been transformed from a sky that was bright blue to one that was filled with large clumps of dark blue and black clouds. Occasionally Bess would see a flash of lightning or hear a rumble of thunder. Yet, for all the activity outside, her eyes always returned to the chicken. She folded her arms and drew in a deep breath as she heard a few strong gusts of wind and could see the trees sway and bend. She could also see the chicken lean in the direction the wind was blowing. However, when the wind subsided, the chicken righted itself again. Was this as strong as the wind would get? Bess began to worry if she and Helen had loosened the stakes enough.

A few seconds later, large droplets of rain began to fall in great abundance. Bess watched the rain and noted how the droplets fell at an angle. The rain came so fast and in such great portions that her view of the chicken began to grow obscured by a gray veil of rain. Bess stood up and made her way over to the window. She stood there, with arms folded, squinting out at the scene of rain and lightning. Suddenly, she could hear the wind grow stronger. She pressed her face close to the glass and now she could see that the chicken was no longer standing up right. In fact, the chicken was lying on its side in the grass.

"Oh dear," Bess said with a slight smile.

She watched as a great gust of wind came along and pushed the chicken off the grass and into the Honey Hills parking lot. Bess bit her lip while she watched the chicken tumble off of a fancy red car before rolling beyond the parking lot and in the direction of a farm. She stepped to the side, straining to see what was going to happen next. The last image she saw was of the chicken bouncing into the fields, head over bottom. Her eyes returned to the now empty patch of grass in front of the Honey Hills Retirement Home. Bess took a deep breath and smiled. Thanks to this storm, she thought, dignity had indeed been returned to the word "retirement" at the Honey Hills Retirement Home.

The following morning, there was no mention of the chicken at the breakfast table. It was one of those mornings where Bess longed for a Honey Hills Newspaper to report on the day's happenings around the center. She walked by the window at the front entrance to Honey Hills. All that was outside was a crisp green patch of grass. The chicken was still gone.

When she got to Bridge Club, she tapped into the next best thing to a Honey Hills Newspaper. Flo Morgenstern had a sense for knowing everything that went on at the Honey Hills Retirement Home. This morning, she did not disappoint Bess.

"Morning, Bess," Flo said when she sat down at the table.

"Flo," Bess smiled. She looked at Rose and Helen who were all but bursting with smiles. "Good morning, ladies. Anyone see a chicken around here?"

"I'm afraid he had a tragic accident," Flo announced. "I heard from some secretary that the chicken landed in Farmer Dray's field where a prized steer took issue with it and punctured it several times with its horns. I'm afraid our poor Mr. Chicken will not be joining us for the chicken barbeque this summer."

"I'm sure someone's upset about that," Rose said.

"I heard Honey Hills wanted Farmer Dray to pay for the chicken to be repaired," Flo reported. "Farmer Dray contended that it was the center's fault for not securing the chicken properly. Neither side budged and so now all that is left is for us to say goodbye to our dear friend Mr. Chicken."

"Can you imagine?" Helen asked with a grin, "not securing something that big to the ground."

"Yes," Bess laughed. "Imagine that."

Bess merely looked across the table at Helen, whose smile was just as big and broad. After a few seconds, Flo noticed the glance being exchanged and spoke up.

"What's so funny?" Flo asked.

"Nothing," Bess quickly answered.

"I think you two know something about this," Flo replied. She pointed her finger at Bess and Helen. "Come on and tell us. What do you know about this chicken thing that we don't know."

It was another one of those moments, Bess thought. One of those moments when she could indulge in yet another school girl habit. The habit of keeping secrets that other people wanted to know. Though she was no longer a school girl, it was still a habit that she continued to indulge in.

GARDEN CANDY

There were two kinds of people that Bess had observed in her nine months at the Honey Hills Retirement Home. There were those people, like herself, who made the effort to watch the news or find a newspaper to read. People like Bess who made an effort to stay engaged with what was going on in the outside world. Whether it be local news, international stories, or even the weather, Bess always chose to keep informed with the events that lay beyond the walls of the Honey Hills Retirement Home.

Bess was also familiar with those Honey Hills residents who didn't care to be as informed. People who didn't care to learn about the latest news or weather for that matter. Somewhere during their stay, these residents seemed to resign themselves to shrinking their life's focus down to just those things that went on at the Honey Hills Retirement Home. The only information that mattered were things like the temperature in the hallway, what was for dinner and what activities were being planned. It was sad, Bess thought, to reach a point in one's life when one no longer cared about the events of the world. When one chose not care to about the world that lay beyond the Honey Hills Retirement Home.

It was for this reason, that Bess forced herself to leave the air conditioned hallways at least once a week to take a walk outside. During the summer months, Bess made a concerted effort to take her walk early in the morning before the heat of the day shown brightly.

Summer mornings usually found Bess walking around the grounds of the Honey Hills Retirement Home where residents lived in small homes that were referred to as "cottages." These "cottages" came with small yards and a small garden where residents were permitted to plant whatever they wanted. When Bess took her summer morning strolls, she enjoyed looking at all the different gardens she passed on her way.

At this time of the year, brightly colored pansies lined a good many of the gardens she saw. Pink, purple and yellow flowers occasionally dotted some of the gardens, mixing with occasional rose bushes or bright white daisies. Bess found herself also taken by the smells that melted on the warm air. The occasional scent that rode under her nose was too sweet to ignore. Sometimes she merely had to stop for a moment and enjoy the scent before resuming her walk.

Some flowers held the occasional scent that brought back good memories of watching her mother work in her garden. On occasion, her mother would wave young Bess over to "smell the garden candy." While Bess didn't have enough money to afford a cottage at the Honey Hills, she could not resist coming out to smell the "garden candy" that was in such sweet abundance.

One of the houses Bess liked to stop at belonged to Marge and Harvey Dent. Bess always enjoyed the dazzling garden at their home. Marge was a recognized Master Gardener, having earned her title after completing a course at a local college. The great pride of her garden were the full red rose bushes that bloomed by the side of the road. They filled the length of her yard and cast an especially sweet aroma for anyone who happened to pass by. Whenever she took her morning walks, Bess would always seek out the road that went by Marge Dent's rose bushes.

"Morning, Bess!" a woman's voice called out.

Bess stopped, looked around one of the bushes, then smiled and waved to Marge. Bess spotted Marge standing next to her garden with a bundle of weeds in one hand and a small gardening tool in the other. Since Bess had moved to the Honey Hills Retirement Home, she and Marge had many discussions on the topic of gardening. It was through their mutual interest in gardening that they became good friends.

This morning, Marge wore a very large hat with a round floppy rim that helped to keep the sun off of her face. Curls of white hair poked out from under the hat. She wore a white short sleeved shirt and a pair of blue jean shorts. Bess immediately looked down at the grass and dirt stains on Marge's knees. To Bess, this was the truest sign that a person was not just a casual gardener. Marge was the kind of gardener who wasn't afraid of getting down on the ground and really mixing it up with the dirt.

"Morning, Marge," Bess said, watching Marge remove her gardening gloves. "The roses have really taken quite nicely this year. You must be very proud."

"I love this time of the year so much," Marge said, her uneven teeth filling a very broad smile. "Every morning I wake up and I just can't wait to find out what my gardens hold for me to see. I would never want to leave my gardens."

"I'm sure your gardens wouldn't want you to leave them," Bess quickly replied.

"Come," Marge said, waving Bess onto the yard. "Let me show you around."

For the next few minutes, Bess carefully followed Marge as she weaved her way around some of her smaller gardens. Bess listened to every detail and sniffed every colorful thing that Marge pointed out. These were the kinds of gardens Bess had always strived for, but was unable to achieve in the small backyard of her house. Indeed, even the garden in the courtyard could not compare to the colors and smells Bess was now experiencing. At one point, Bess had to shake her head after being filled with such sweet aromas. Suddenly Bess noticed that Marge's eyes were moving away from the flowers and towards the road. There she saw her husband, Harvey, walking up the street in his tan pants and button down shirt.

"Here he comes," Marge sighed, dropping her gardening shovel.

Bess watched as Marge made her way over to the street. She reached out to Harvey, taking his hand and giving him a kiss on the cheek. She watched Marge follow Harvey into the house, then return to where Bess was standing. Bess could see that Marge's carefree demeanor had changed in just a matter of seconds. Marge's eyes were looking down. Her smile was gone.

"Is something wrong?" Bess finally asked.

"Oh it's…it's nothing I guess," Marge mumbled.

Bess let the silence linger. She knew that sometimes people were more prone to speak after a spell of silence, as opposed to being pressed for a response.

"It's Harvey," Marge finally said, causing Bess to smile just a little at her strategy.

"Every morning for fifty-one years, Harvey has taken a walk before breakfast. It has been his routine to wake up before the sun and get dressed to go. I've never interrupted that routine because Harvey is just the best man I know. We've been married for fifty-one years. Never once have I seen Harvey even glance at another woman. The last couple of weeks I've noticed that when he comes home from his walks…I can smell perfume on him."

"Perfume?" Bess asked. Suddenly she was less aware of the flowers and the scents around her. She could feel her instincts rise like a tide demanding attention. Her focus was no longer on the gardens, but on Marge and the words she used to describe this little mystery that had just presented itself to Bess.

"Yes, I said perfume," Marge nodded. "I can't really follow him because of my arthritis in my hip. He walks too fast for me. I really don't believe he's cheating on me after all these years, but I must admit the thought has crossed my mind."

"Have you confronted him about the smell?" Bess asked.

"I've tried," Marge sighed. "Harvey's having a little trouble with his speech these days. What he says sometimes doesn't make much sense to me."

"I see," Bess responded. "Would you like me to follow him for you?"

"Would you?" Marge asked.

"Of course," Bess said. "I usually take my walks in the morning, like Harvey."

"It wouldn't be an inconvenience?" Marge asked.

"I walk every day," Bess explained. "It wouldn't be an inconvenience, Marge."

"Thank you," Marge said, her uneven toothy smile returning to her face. "It would be such a load off my mind to know what is happening."

As she smiled and went on to make small talk about Harvey and her gardens, Bess began to think about the promise she had just committed herself to. Would she really be able to keep up with Harvey on one of his long walks? What should she do if she found him with another woman? Bess thought about these questions all through the evening. Then, right before she fell asleep one more question slipped into her mind. Was this something a retired person would do?

A GARDEN'S WORTH

The next morning, Bess found herself waking up and going out for a walk much earlier than her normal routine. Marge had warned Bess that Harvey was prone to starting his walks well before the sun was up. When Bess stepped out of the Honey Hills Retirement Home, a deep hue of dark blue filled the sky. A light dew was spread over the grass. The sun was not yet visible, but the morning sky made it quite possible for Bess to make out details when she walked.

As far as she could tell, she was the only walker out on the streets. When she arrived at the corner to the street where Marge and Harvey lived, Bess stopped and waited. She thought about how silent it was this early in the morning. Not even the sound of chirping birds could be heard while she stood and waited. Then, she saw the lamp next to the Dent's driveway turn on. A second later, she saw Harvey appear from the front door and walk down the driveway. He started out with a quick pace as he moved into the street. Bess stepped from the corner and began to follow Harvey on his walk.

While she trailed behind him, Bess was struck by the remarkable similarity of the homes that lined the streets to the Honey Hills property. Most every home was a red brick, one story ranch home. The only deviation in design was in the yards, where she saw some gardens, some lawn chairs and one gnome with a pleasant smile painted on his face.

Harvey kept a brisk pace and Bess found herself hoping that he wasn't going to take a very long walk. Her right knee was feeling stiff, perhaps not used to walking this fast this early in the day.   Harvey's pace was unrelenting and unhesitating. While Bess used walks as a way to admire her surroundings, think about things, or just enjoy the day, it was becoming clear to her that Harvey was doing none of these things.   He was out for physical exercise, plain and simple. While following his route, Bess walked by some beautiful gardens and some lovely flowers. She was tempted to stop more than once, but she promised Marge she would follow Harvey.   A promise that she intended to keep.

After nearly an hour, Bess watched as Harvey had followed the streets in such a way that he had made a complete circle and was now heading back to his home. He had done a remarkable walk of twists and turns throughout the development that stretched around the grounds of the Honey Hills Retirement Home.   As he approached the street where he lived, Bess watched as Harvey came to a complete stop in the middle of the street. It was the first time he had stopped all morning. Bess also stopped, placed her hand on her hip and began to catch her breath. She was breathing harder than she normally would for a walk, but keeping up with Harvey was clearly no small task. Now she stood by the side of the road and watched Harvey's head turn left, then right, then left again. He reached up and adjusted the glasses that had slid down the slop of his nose.

"Is he lost?" Bess asked herself.

Finally, Harvey made a right and walked down a street that stretched in the opposite direction of his home. This was clearly not the right way to go, Bess thought. If Harvey was having an affair, this would be the ideal time of the day to have it. It was still early in the morning and no one was awake to watch him.

Suddenly, Harvey veered off the road and onto a front yard. He marched with great conviction through the grass and right up to the front porch of a house. However, instead of going directly to the door, as Bess had expected him to do, Harvey sat down on a large white wooden bench on the front porch. He eased himself down into the bench, breathing hard, and sat there for a few minutes. Bess was uncertain just what to do. Should she walk up and confront Harvey? Should she strike up a conversation, and not accuse him of anything? Perhaps she should start a conversation with Harvey to see where it would lead? It had been a long time since she spoke to Harvey, but Bess thought he might remember her.

As she was about to step into the yard, Bess saw the front door open and a woman appeared. The woman had white hair that shone even brighter now that the morning sun was up. Dressed in tan pants and a long-sleeved white shirt, the woman walked up to where Harvey was sitting. She stood in front of him, talking to him and then pointing out to the street. When the woman finished talking, she slowly sat down on the large white bench beside Harvey. Bess watched as the woman wrapped her arm around Harvey's shoulder and patted him with her hand.

Bess noticed that Harvey really didn't respond much to the woman's gesture. There was no kiss. No hand holding. Instead there was Harvey sitting and staring down at his feet. After a minute, Bess found it ridiculous to be standing in the street watching the events unfold. She stepped into the grass and followed the same path Harvey made up to the front porch. The closer she got, the more she began to smell a distinctly strong brand of perfume coming from the woman beside Harvey. Bess suspected it was the perfume Marge had commented about.

"Good morning," Bess said with a smile. It was the only thing she could think of to say to disarm an otherwise embarrassing situation.

"Do you know her, Harvey?" the woman asked.

Harvey looked at Bess and mumbled something under his breath. The words he spoke were either too soft or too mangled for Bess to understand. His eyes stared at her, his eye brows tilted to the sides, and finally he smiled. He reached out with his hand and grabbed Bess by the arm.

"Heh...heh...hello, Bess," Harvey managed to say in a way that Bess thought was half- nervous and half-stuttering.

"Hello, Harvey," Bess said. She knelt down, wincing at the discomfort in her stiff right knee. "Why are you here?"

"Th...this...is...my home," Harvey managed to answer.

"Now, sweetie," the woman behind him said, rubbing her hand on his back. The woman looked up at Bess and smiled with bright red lips. "Me and Harvey go through this every morning. Old Harvey parks himself right here on my bench and insists that this is his home. I come out here and sit with Harvey. We talk a little and then he leaves and goes to his home. I asked him where he lives, but he can't really talk too good. He can't tell me his address. I can't even get a last name out of Harvey. You know his last name?"

"Harvey Dent," Bess quickly said. "His wife's name is Marge Dent. They live right down the street from you."

"Oh, yes," the woman replied with a snap of her fingers. "I know Marge. She sold me this beautiful bench a few weeks ago. I didn't know Harvey was gonna come with the bench, though."

"Harvey," Bess said, leaning in close. "Should we go home to Marge?"

"Okay," Harvey quietly answered. He stood up and Bess led Harvey home. On their way back, Bess made a concerted effort to be the one to set the pace for this particular walk.

When they returned to Harvey's street, Bess asked Harvey a few questions. She tried to make some conversation with him, but her questions were left hanging with little comment or no reply. Eventually Harvey chose to simply grow silent, electing not to say anything while they walked. As they approached the house, Bess saw Marge tending to the rose bushes closest to the road. The moment she made eye contact with Bess, Marge removed her floppy hat and put down the gardening tools. She clapped her hands together then folded her arms and walked down to meet Harvey and Bess by the side of the road.

"Have a good walk?" Marge asked.

Harvey nodded at the question. He didn't make eye contact with Bess or Marge when he responded.

"I have breakfast on the table for you," Marge said, gently turning Harvey towards the door. "Go in and eat."

Harvey mumbled something under his breath and walked away. Bess again thought it sounded like a mish mash of words that were being spoken too softly and too closely together to make sense.

"Where was he?" Marge asked, turning to Bess.

"I followed him around the development for a good bit before he stopped at a house just a few blocks away from here," Bess reported. "It seems there's a lady living there who bought a bench from you not so long ago. I believe Harvey still thinks the bench is in front of *his* house. It's an easy mistake, since all these homes look the same."

"Yes," Marge nodded. She took a deep breath, turned and walked back to her gardens. "Unfortunately he's been making that mistake more than once. I've been finding things he lays down in the oddest places. One night he got up in the pitch black darkness and insisted it was time for his walk. It wasn't even half past midnight when he woke up and started getting dressed. It took a lot for me to get him back into bed."

"That doesn't sound very safe," Bess said.

"Well, he is stronger than me," Marge explained with a smile. "I can't very well physically stop him from doing anything, but he listens to me."

"He seems to have trouble talking," Bess observed. "That plus his confusion. Marge, have you spoken to anyone at Honey Hills about this situation?"

"Not really," Marge replied. She reached up and wiped some sweat off her face. "He always manages to find his way back home when he goes for his walks. As for that bench I sold Mrs. Crockett, I'll call her today and buy it back. I'll pay double what she did so she can feel good about the profit. When I get that bench back it should make it easier for Harvey to find his way home."

"And what about Harvey?" Bess pressed. "I do think you should talk to someone. His confusion may be something that is correctable."

"It's Alzheimer's," Marge said in a very clear tone. "Harvey's father had it. My daughter's a nurse and she said he's in the early stages."

"Oh, dear," Bess said. She took a step closer to Marge. "I'm so sorry, Marge. Have you started to make arrangements for Harvey?"

"Not yet," Marge said. "I want him to enjoy being home for as long as he can."

"They have an excellent program for Alzheimer patients at Honey Hills," Bess said. "I've walked by there and seen them throwing ball, playing music, doing card games, really trying anything to stimulate the brain. I think Harvey would love it there."

"That may be so," Marge said, her eyes turning away from Bess. "I understand the Honey Hills' rules here are very clear about not splitting up couples. You see, if Harvey moves into the main building, which is where Alzheimer's patients go, than I must also move there with him."

Bess noticed how Marge's eyes were now lingering over her garden. She watched Marge slowly shake her head.

"I just can't part with my flowers, Bess," Marge said in a firm tone. "I won't let some- thing like that come between me and my gardens. I need to think about my flowers, too, in making such a decision. Right now, my flowers need me and I need them."

With those final words, Bess watched Marge turn and go back to tending to her roses. As she trimmed and pruned, Bess slowly began to walk down to the street to walk back to her room. When she walked by the Dent's house, Bess could see Harvey sitting on a chair next to the window. His head was turned to the side. His eyes fixed on nothing in particular. His mouth hung open.

Bess looked back once more at Marge, who was now smiling from ear to ear while she cut and sculpted a bush next to her garden. As she walked back to her room, Bess now realized that it took more than sunshine and rain to make Marge's garden the most beautiful in all the Honey Hills' grounds. It also appeared to be requiring the welfare and safety of her husband. Bess only hoped that she would never choose the lives of her flowers over the life of her Harvey.

NURTURE AND GROW

A few weeks later, Bess met Samantha at the Honey Hills' multipurpose room. It was the annual Flower Fest, a show put on every summer by the Honey Hills Retirement Home. In attendance, Bess and Samantha found some of the Honey Hills' best gardeners with a few of their most prized plants on display. Bess noticed how each gardener beamed from ear to ear while watching people admire the plants they had labored so hard to nurture and grow during the summer. Some where deep inside, Bess wished she could be one of those gardeners.

When Samantha and Bess walked by a table where Marge Dent had a few of her brilliant red roses on display, Bess smiled and nodded to Marge. A few minutes later, Bess quietly turned to Samantha and told her the story of Marge, Harvey, and the garden that Marge felt needed her more than her husband. When she finished the story, Bess could see a look of disapproval move over Samantha's face. Her eyes narrowed and her lips pushed together. Bess was curious to hear what Samantha would say.

"That's terrible," Samantha hissed, her eyes flicking back at Marge. "What kind of a wife would do something like that?"

"Samantha," Bess sighed, turning to look across the room at Marge. "She's trying to give him a chance to fight. She may want him to enjoy his independence a bit longer, too. When he gets moved into a full care facility, he'll be watched around the clock by nurses. There'll be no privacy left for him then."

"Someone with problems like that *needs* constant attention," Samantha observed. "She should have him there instead of putting it off."

"Of course you would say that," Bess mumbled with a disapproving stare.

"I think I'm right," Samantha said. She paused and looked at Bess. "Don't you think she's doing the wrong thing?"

"At this stage in life," Bess began, "your spouse is not just some task that needs to be completed. You're not looking at socks that need to be sewn or a floor that needs mopping. You're talking about someone's partner for life, Samantha. There are…emotions involved. I'm sure she's doing the best she can."

"I just think she should want what's best for him," Samantha replied.

"Perhaps giving him a chance to fight a disease *is* what's best for him," Bess offered.

"All I'm saying is he needs to be cared for," Samantha stated. "He needs nurses round the clock and he needs to be kept somewhere safe."

"That's what you said about your father," Bess said turning and staring at her daughter. Her words caused a small measure of silence to follow.

"What about Daddy?" Samantha finally asked, stepping closer to Bess.

"Soon after his illness," Bess recalled looking around for a moment, "you were very quick to have your father sign one of those papers you gave me the other day."

"Daddy was in bad shape," Samantha recalled. "Someone had to take care of him." Bess barely noticed the beautiful white lily on the table next to where she was standing. Her eyes and her total focus were on Samantha, who looked at Bess with the same wide-eyed expression she had as a child.

"You're father was fine when he signed that paper," Bess said. "The day you started having that nurse come around...well, that's when he started to die."

"Mom!" Samantha objected, quickly looking around to see if anyone heard her. Samantha stepped closer to Bess and whispered, "He had cancer."

"My mother had cancer," Bess said. "She wasn't supposed to live, but she fought it and survived another five years. When that nurse started coming to our house, telling your father to stay in bed, getting things for him, filling him with all kinds of medicine, well, it just took the fight out of him."

"Mom, he was sick," Samantha said firmly.

"People have fought off illnesses," Bess continued. "You're father could have fought off his cancer for a year. Instead, that nurse just helped him make his peace with God much earlier than he should have. Much earlier than I wanted him to. I'm not going to let you do that to me, Samantha. When I grow sick, I'm going to fight for my life with every fiber in my body. I don't want a nurse keeping me in bed. I don't want people to get things for me. Now you can tell your lawyer I'm not interested in signing his paper. You tell him what I said. See if he can come up with something in writing that'll make us both happy."

Samantha stood silent in front of Bess for a moment. Neither knew what to say. Bess was barely aware of the people moving around them. She looked closely and could see a tear appear from the corner of Samantha's one eye. Bess wanted to say something. It was her instinct as a mother to try and heal hurt feelings. Before she could speak, Samantha quickly turned and left the Flower Fest in tears.

A FEELING LIKE HOME

Dance class had become very awkward for Bess. What was once an enjoyable day of the week had now become the morning she looked forward to the least. After helping Chet solve the mystery of Bart the therapy dog, the relationship between Chet and Bess had changed. She could sense it on the dance floor. She could feel it in the halls when she couldn't bring her eyes to look at him when he passed by her.

Creating the tension for Bess was how concerned Chet was that she would be seen leaving his room when she stayed there. How concerned he was about *his* reputation, and how *her* reputation was never mentioned. It bothered Bess to see this side of him. A side that was more self-centered than the gentleman she had come to expect on the dance floor.

Still, Bess decided to continue with dance class. She genuinely enjoyed dancing, and for that she would always be grateful to Chet. He was the one who suggested she come to the club's meetings shortly after she moved to Honey Hills. He was the one who would stay after the meetings to help her master a new a step or a tricky move. He was the one who would always select her as his partner.

Lately, they still danced but his eyes didn't linger on her the way they used to. His grip on her hand was a little tighter, not as gentle and soft as it had been. Even when they passed in the hallway, there were moments when she could sense he couldn't even bring himself to make eye contact. On one occasion, a quick "hello" was all she had received in the days since she helped him recover his wallet.

Sitting on her chair in her room, reflecting on Chet's behavior, Bess turned to a picture of her husband framed on the small table next to the window. Her eyes lingered on the black and white photo and she smiled.

"No need to be jealous," she said to the photograph. "I don't love him. I just feel badly that in trying to help someone…I think I've ruined a friendship."

Her husband merely smiled at her words and remained silent. She often thought that having a picture there was the next best thing to having her husband still alive. When he was alive, and she would share her thoughts, he would simply greet her words with a silent reply. Sometimes he would smile. Sometimes he'd just sigh. Sometimes he'd mumble a few words and walk away. She often joked with him about how he was like John Wayne in one of her favorite movies, *The Quiet Man.* Even in the final days before his death, he didn't use his words to convey his true feelings for her. It was in his dark eyes. In the way he held her hands. In the way he reached up and stroked her hair and caressed her cheek. To Bess, his actions on his death bed spoke volumes to her about his love for her.

"Bess?" a voice asked, cracking her door open.

Bess blinked a few times, as if waking up from some type of dream. She moved her eyes from her husband's picture and focused on the door to her room.

"Yes," Bess managed to say, "come in."

The door opened wider to reveal a woman from her dance club. Her name was Matilda Dower. She was tall, with long legs that made Bess think she must have been an athlete when she was younger. Matilda was also hunched over, with a slight hump where her back was located. No doubt, Bess reasoned, the effects of a bone disease quite common in women called osteoporosis. She'd seen other women with the same appearance. Bess was impressed that Matilda never let her disposition get her down. She kept a busy schedule, always had a smile ready, and loved to dance.

"Good morning," Matilda said, walking into the room.

"Hello, Matilda," Bess said, pointing over to a chair next to where she was sitting. "This is a nice surprise. Unexpected company is always a surprise in the morning. Did I forget about dance class?"

"No," Matilda said with a wave of her hand. "This has nothing to do with dance, all though you and Chet are very smooth when you dance together. I love watching you two dance. You always look so graceful together, like two swans."

"Thank you," Bess said, feeling her face grow flushed. "Chet is really the better dancer. I just try to keep up with him."

"Don't be so modest," Matilda replied, removing her eye glasses. She pulled out a tissue from her shirt sleeve and began to clean her glasses. "You really are very good, too."

Bess always found it hard to take a compliment. She was more comfortable giving them out than receiving them. She could toss out a hundred compliments a day, but when one came her way she usually managed to side step it. She wasn't sure why. It was something that her husband pointed out to her. He noticed how whenever he paid her a compliment for her appearance, the way she handled Samantha, or even her meals, she would always find something else to take the credit. The memory caused her to glance over at his picture to see his smiling face again.

"So why are you here?" Bess finally asked, turning her eyes back to her guest.

"Chet wanted me to tell you that he feels terrible for what he said or did to you," Matilda explained.

"Matilda, does he know what he did? Does he *really* know?" Bess asked.

"I don't think so," Matilda laughed. "He reminds me of my husband. He only notices the obvious and misses the little things. Right now, what is obvious to him, I guess, is how you've changed when you're around him. That's why I'm here this morning."

"Have you been sent to apologize for him?" Bess asked.

"Yes," Matilda nodded. "Chet asked me to do just that."

"Tell him I will only accept an apology from the person giving it," Bess quickly announced. "Tell him I will be reading outside in the Japanese garden this evening. If he has something to say, he may come there to say it."

Later that day, Bess sat alone on a bench in the midst of a small Japanese garden that bordered the west end of the Honey Hills Retirement Home. The sky was dark blue. The sun was large and red and sagged at the sides as it drifted into the horizon. Though the faint evening light was hard to read by, Bess continued to try her best to work on a book of crossword puzzles. She usually spent an hour a day on a crossword puzzle. She enjoyed the challenge and liked to keep her mind sharp.

Soon after moving into Honey Hills, Bess found that the comforts of Honey Hills made it difficult to keep her mind active. Everyone was so nice and so willing to do everything; Bess often felt that one could pretty much go through an entire day without making any conscious decisions whatsoever. The nurses at Honey Hills were more than ready to try to control and direct every resident, whether the residents liked it or not

Bess looked up from her book just in time to see Chet step into the walkway that wound around the garden. He was wearing a white, short sleeved sports shirt, light blue pants, and white shoes. His hands were in his pockets. He looked down at his shoes while he walked, then looked up at Bess and smiled.

"Fine evening," Chet said, easing himself down on the bench beside her.

"It is," Bess answered, closing her book.

Chet sat for a moment, looking at the flowers directly across from them. He stayed quiet for a moment, then turned his head up to the sky.

"I'm sorry for what's happened between us," Chet said in a soft voice. "You just don't seem as happy with me, and I've been rattling my brain trying to figure out what I said or did to make you mad. I don't know what is, but I'm truly sorry anyway."

"I'm not mad," Bess quickly said, folding her hands on her lap. "No, it's not that I'm mad. I'm just…disappointed."

"How have I disappointed you, Bess?" Chet asked, leaning forward to get a better look at her. His blue eyes focused on her face, waiting for her to speak.

"I'm afraid I just had this…idea of you in my head," Bess explained. "A perfect gentleman on the dance floor. A perfect gentleman to smile and say "hi" to in the hallways. I'm afraid I let my imagination fill in the rest and it left me with this perfect image of you. I am afraid I set myself up for disappointment, Chet."

"Well, I'm quite certain I must have done something to set the wheels in motion," Chet said, biting his lip for a second. "I am sorry. I hope that things can go back to the way they were for us. Back to smiling on the dance floor. Back to smiles between us."

"There will be more smiles," Bess nodded. "It is a problem I have thought a great deal about. At first, I thought you were to blame for how I felt. After giving it some thought, I realized that I was actually the one to blame."

Bess took a deep breath. She leaned back and let her eyes come to rest on a small patch of daisies to her side. Her eyes moved and locked on a monarch butterfly that was weaving and bobbing around some flowers. She soaked up the scene of the butterfly and the flowers and smiled.

"Is it not good to have a place like this to live?" Bess asked, looking around. "A place where you actually have time to stop and think about things? I sometimes feel badly when I see my daughter in here. She's so busy checking her watch and checking her cell phone. Time for her is not in great abundance, as is true for a lot of young people. In this place, at our age Chet, we are truly fortunate to have free time to stop and to think."

"Yes, it is," Chet answered. He took a deep breath and looked Bess in the eye. "Is there anything I can do? Anything to help patch things up between us?"

"Well, there may be one thing," Bess said, clearing her throat. She looked down at her hands on her lap and began to speak. "I have a birthday coming up soon. I've been looking for someone to take an airplane ride with me."

"Are you going somewhere?" Chet asked.

"No, no," Bess answered. "I've rented a small plane to take me up for my birthday. It'll just be a flight around the valley. I remember you once told me you flew planes during the war. Would you consider going up in a plane with me?"

"No," Chet quickly answered. He paused for a few seconds and Bess could feel her face turn red. "I don't have to *consider* it because I don't have to think about it. Of course I'll go up with you. It would be my honor to be with you to celebrate your birthday."

"Thank you," Bess said, feeling a sense of relief run through her body.

Chet smiled and sat back in his seat. He slid across the bench, moving a bit closer to her.

She could feel her heart begin to beat a little faster. He reached over and took her hand in his much larger hand. Together they sat, hand in hand, watching the stars begin to poke through the purple veil of evening. As she sat, Bess could not ignore the feeling she had while holding Chet's soft, gentle hand. The feeling of being home after a long time away.

BINGO

When she sat down with her friends for Tuesday morning bridge, Bess could not help but smile at her cards. They weren't particularly good cards, but she didn't care. Her mind was still thinking about Chet and their evening sitting outside watching the stars come out. She could still see Chet holding her hand under the stars. It truly was the best way to end a day, Bess thought. She was barely aware of her cards when she heard someone clear their throat.

"I believe there is a conspiracy going on at Bingo night," Flo Morgenstern announced to the other members of the Tuesday morning Bridge Club.

Bess ignored the comment. She was happy about Chet and she didn't want the feeling to end. She looked at her cards and began to think about how to play them. Rose Grumbine and Helen Gruber joined Bess in her interest for how this particular round was going to play out. While they drew cards, checked their hands, and kept their minds focused on the game, Bess again heard Flo speak.

"Someone is winning unfairly at Bingo."

Again, her words were met with silence.

"I've sat with you at a Bingo table," Helen finally chimed in. "The only person you think doesn't cheat at Bingo is you."

"I'm not the best loser, I'll admit that much," Flo said, drumming her fingers on the table. "What's been happening at Bingo night in the dining hall can only be described as cheating."

"So who is the cheater?" Helen asked.

"Lilly Shumocker," Flo quickly replied without hesitation. "She's had at least one Bingo each week for the last eight weeks."

"How on earth do you know that?" Rose finally spoke up.

"Bingo night is once a week," Flo explained. "When I return to my room after Bingo I keep records of which players won for that particular night. Then the following week I'll sit next to one of the winners to see if I can get any tips from them on how to play better."

"You keep records?" Helen asked, lowering her cards and rolling her eyes.

"Yes," Flo continued. "The only person who has had a Bingo for the last eight weeks in a row has been Lily Shumocker. Mind you, different people have also won from week to week, but she's the only person who's won every week. I've sat at her table. I've sat right beside her on one occasion. I keep a closer eye on her than I do my own Bingo card. I cannot figure out how she's doing it, but I'm quite certain that she is cheating, but I don't know how."

Silence followed Flo's statement. Bess remained focused on her cards. When she finally pulled a card from her hand she noticed that everyone around the table was looking at her.

"What?" Bess asked.

"Aren't you going to help?" Flo asked.

"Help with what?" Bess asked, turning to Flo. "As far as I can tell you simply want to accuse someone of being a cheater. Why do you need my help to do that?"

"You helped Chet," Rose spoke up.

"That was different," Bess said. She sat up in her seat beginning to realize she would need to offer an explanation behind her decision not to help Flo. "There were things being taken from Chet's room. There was a crime being committed. There is no crime when it comes to winning Bingo."

"Come with me," Flo urged, drumming her narrow fingers on the table. "Next Bingo game is tonight. Come and see if she wins for the ninth week in a row."

"Oh my," Bess sighed with a wave of her hand. She smiled at Flo and tried to downplay the conflict between them. "I'm not really interested in playing Bingo, Flo. I'm also not interested in calling someone a cheat, either. I like Lily. She's always been very nice to me when I see her in the halls. Besides, I don't want to spend my retirement solving one mystery after another. Sounds a bit like work to me. Retirement should mean having leisure days to spend doing fun things, not investigating mysteries."

"You once said you had a first class mind," Flo pressed, speaking in a louder tone. "Does it make sense to you that Lily is the only person winning from one week to the next? Eight weeks is a long time. What does your first class mind think about something like that?"

The words caused Bess to think about the situation. In her mind, the odds of it being a coincidence were truly remote. Yet, Bess began to wonder how one would cheat at Bingo?

"If you come and I win a round," Flo began, and then paused for a few seconds. "I'll…I'll let you pick out a prize from the prize tray. Now how could you call that a bad deal?"

BINGO CHIPS AND CHEATS

Later that evening, Bess arrived in the Dining Hall to find a room full of ladies seated around ten large tables. When she walked in the room the smell of meatloaf and mashed potatoes was still lingering in the air from dinner. Bess took a few steps before stopping under a golden chandelier that cast narrow streams of light around the room. She carefully scanned the room, looking at the many faces. She quickly spotted Flo standing up and waving her arms for Bess to see.

"She's not too subtle," Bess mumbled to herself.

As she made her way through the room, Bess could sense her instincts guiding her eyes over the faces of some of the players in attendance. The Bingo players who looked serious to her came with special markers to mark their cards and special wipes to wipe the cards clean after each game. They also held no expression on their faces, kept their hands clenched by their cards, and appeared ready to play at a second's notice.

Looking at such serious Bingo players made Bess smile a little. For these ladies, Bess reasoned, Bingo was the one thing in their life they could get excited about. Wasn't that what life was about, Bess thought. Life should be about getting excited about something from time to time. When she finally sat down next to Flo, Bess had a greater understanding and appreciation for Flo's excitement about Bingo.

"About time you got here," Flo grumbled when Bess reached her. "It gets hard to save a seat. I had to fight off a few ladies to keep this chair for you."

"Thank you, Flo," Bess quietly said, sitting down.

"I believe you know everyone," Flo said, gesturing to the other ladies at the table.

Bess smiled and glanced around the table at some familiar faces seated there. When her eyes looked to the side, she noticed she was seated next to none other than Lilly Shumocker.

Lilly was about ten years younger than Bess. She was one of the youngest residents at Honey Hill. Her hair was a mix of gray with some dark streaks still visible. Her face was not filled with the wrinkles and cracks that lined the faces of the older residents. What Bess quickly noticed about Lilly after a few chance meetings was her constant habit of chewing gum. She noticed it when she passed Lilly in the hallway. She noticed it when she saw Lilly talking to other residents. She even noticed it when Lilly ate dinner. Bess observed how Lilly never took the gum out of her mouth. She was amazed how Lilly was able to chew and swallow her dinner every night without removing her gum.

"Hello, Bess," Lilly said, sliding a Bingo card over to her. "You'll need one of these if you're going to play."

"Oh that's okay," Bess said, shaking her head at the offer of a card.

"Well, why are you here if you're not going to play?" Lilly asked.

"She doesn't come here very often," Flo quickly said, handing Bess a Bingo card and some chips. "She's going to play. Thanks, Lilly."

"That's right," Bess laughed with a shrug of her shoulders. "I haven't played Bingo in a long time. Maybe I forgot I needed a card."

"I'll help you out," Lilly grinned before making her gum crack in her mouth.

Bess turned to see Flo's eyebrows go up after hearing Lilly's offer.

"This should be easy," Flo whispered to Bess.

Bess turned to her Bingo card, placed a chip on the free spot, then felt a hand on her shoulder. She looked at Lilly, who was also arranging her cards. Bess turned in her seat to see the hand on her shoulder belonged to Alice Wetbottom.

A tall, heavy woman with hair that extended out in all directions, Alice was one of the more recognizable figures at Honey Hills. With her broad gray mane of hair framing her small face, Alice was one of the first residents Bess could remember because of her unusual appearance.

"Is everyone ready to play?" Alice asked.

"I think so," Bess said, trying not to stare at the stray locks of hair that spilled out from Alice's head. "Are you also playing Bingo this evening, Alice?"

"I'm in charge of Bingo this year," Alice replied. "I coordinate the gift donations from the churches. I also schedule the dates with the dining hall. The part I like is calling the numbers. It's fun to be the center of attention every week, if only for an hour."

Bess smiled at the comment and watched Alice begin to walk away. As she walked, Bess could see Alice's eyes linger for a few seconds to the side of Bess, where Lilly was seated. Bess wondered what Alice was staring at, but before Bess could ask Alice had walked away.

A few seconds later, Bess watched Alice move to the front of the room. She clapped her hands, and spoke in a loud tone,

"Good evening, ladies!" Alice announced in a clear direct tone. "Before we begin I would like to welcome Ruth Moore here tonight. Ruth will be turning one hundred years old soon. Let's all clap for Ruth."

The words were followed by a few seconds of loud clapping. Bess turned her head a few times in her seat until she could see whom she guessed was Ruth Moore, a small woman with white curls and a warm smile on her face. Ruth seemed to enjoy the moment. She smiled and simply waved at the many ladies clapping for her.

Bess then watched as Alice cleared her throat, leaned over a microphone, and called out the first letter and number for the game.

"The first one is B-7," her voice rang out in the dining hall.

For the next few minutes, Bess carefully listened and played her card. She also looked over and kept one eye on Lilly's Bingo card. She noticed that Lilly had already laid out two chips on her card. As the numbers continued, Bess looked up front and watched Alice. She noticed how Alice moved her head from side to side, first picking a number and then looking to place the number somewhere.

"O-66," Alice called out.

Bess checked her card and quickly glanced over at Lilly, who was now grinning and placing another chip on her card.

"C'mon," she heard Lilly say to her card. She looked over at Bess and laughed, perhaps embarrassed at having someone overhear her talking to her card.

As she looked at Lilly, Bess realized she was doing nothing wrong with how she played. No, Bess thought, if there was someone using underhanded tactics, she now suspected the person responsible with calling the numbers.

"Has Alice called the numbers for the last few weeks?" Bess asked.

"Alice *always* calls the numbers," Flo replied while staring at her card.

Bess quickly stood up, realizing that time was of the essence. Lilly was very close to getting her Bingo and she wanted to get to the front of the room before it happened.

She heard another number and letter called as she made her way to the front of the room.

"BINGO!" she heard Lilly's voice call out.

When Bess reached the front of the room, Alice looked over at her with an unwelcoming glance. Bess smiled and stood with her hands behind her back.

"Just wanted to see what your job was like," Bess said, looking down at the hopper of balls Alice was turning to pull out each ball with letters and numbers on it. It appeared to Bess that when she did this, Alice then placed the ball on a large board that helped her keep track of all the letters and numbers she had called.

"Lilly!" Alice called out. "Read off your BINGO, please."

Bess watched Alice quickly begin to pick up the balls while Lilly called out the letters and numbers that made up her Bingo. It appeared to Bess that Alice wasn't even checking the balls. At one point, Bess heard Lilly call out a number but Alice couldn't locate the ball that matched what Lilly had.

"That's correct! That's right! Got that one!" Alice called out, barely glancing at the balls while she quickly tossed them back into the hopper.

"Shouldn't you be checking those?" Bess asked.

"Heaven's no," Alice smiled. "It's about having fun! Making people feel good! I don't do this to disappoint people."

Bess smiled after hearing Alice offer her explanation. As she watched Alice put the last of the balls back in the hopper, Bess looked at what appeared to be writing on Alice's hand. She couldn't tell exactly what it was and needed a better look. Bess quickly reached down and picked up a ball from the tray.

"Here," Bess said, handing the ball to Alice.

When Alice reached out for it, Bess quickly grabbed her hand and turned it to get a better view. There she spotted numbers, Lilly's Bingo numbers, written on Alice's hand. She then placed the ball in Alice's hand and gave her a knowing look.

"Tomorrow, after breakfast, may I stop by your room to talk?" Bess asked.

Alice quietly nodded. Together their eyes turned to the rest of the ladies patiently waiting for the next round of Bingo to begin. Lilly was helping herself to a prize from the prize table. When Bess walked back to her seat, she gave Lilly a pat on her shoulder and a sincere "congratulations." On the other side of where she was seated, Flo was nervously tapping her chip on the table and staring at Bess. Finally, she leaned close to Bess and whispered in her ear,

"She won again!" Flo whispered. "She must be a cheater!"

"Tomorrow," Bess said. "I'll tell you tomorrow."

ALICE'S ADMISSION

A fish tank. It was the first thing that caught Bess's eye when she entered Alice's room right after breakfast had been served. Bess was reminded of her daughter, Samantha, who used to have a fish tank in her bedroom when she was younger. For Bess, it brought back memories of being a young mother. Memories of days filled with playing games and going places with Samantha. Memories of grilled cheese sandwich lunches and favorite books to read before bed. Memories of checking on Samantha at bedtime before pausing long enough to listen to the soothing sounds of her fish tank. The sounds of the tank combined with the easy motions of the fish always helped Bess unwind at the end of many a hectic day. Years later, Bess now turned her eyes away from the fish tank and the memories it rekindled. Her attention now centered on the woman seated in front of her.

"So you know my dirty little secret?" Alice asked, rubbing her chin.

"I'm not sure what I know," Bess replied. "I understand Lilly has won at Bingo for a few weeks in a row. A friend of mine had suspected her of manipulating the games in her favor, but after I watched her play yesterday I concluded she couldn't possibly be doing it."

"Lilly isn't doing anything wrong!" Alice stated in an angry voice. She sat back in her seat and nervously ran her hand over her gray hair.

"I know," Bess quietly said. "I suspected it was you when I walked up to where you were standing. When I saw the numbers on your hand, it simply confirmed those suspicions. Weren't you afraid of someone else walking up and doing what I did? Weren't you afraid that someone would come up to your table and see that you were cheating?"

"All the ladies who attend Bingo nights are there simply to play," Alice replied. "They don't come to observe like you. They don't come with suspicions. They come to stare at their cards and chat with their friends. In the months I've been calling Bingo, you're the first person who was less concerned with playing Bingo and more concerned with watching me."

"So why are you doing it?" Bess finally asked. She leaned forward in her seat. "Why are you helping Lilly win?"

"She's a friend," Alice answered. She looked down at her hands which had moved from her hair to tugging at a white tissue on her lap. "She's a friend who is dying."

The words caught Bess by surprise. She sat back in her seat and took a deep breath. The idea that the youngest person at Honey Hills was dying took her by surprise.

"Are you sure?" Bess asked.

"Lung cancer," Alice replied. "Lilly used to be a very heavy smoker. She told me they found a spot on her lung that grew from her last checkup. They did a test on it and found that it was indeed an aggressive form of cancer. The doctors say she has maybe two months."

"My goodness," Bess sighed. The idea that someone would look you in the eye and tell you how much of your life you had left was the kind of news Bess never wanted to receive. When she died, she hoped it would be sudden and quick. She liked the idea of being able to look down the road at life, and not be told the kind of news that Lilly had to hear.

"As I told you last night," Alice said. "What I try to do on Bingo night is have fun and make people feel good. I want to give Lilly something positive to focus on each week even if it's something as small as Bingo. I think a little happiness each week is a fair thing for someone condemned to death, don't you?"

"I agree," Bess said with a quick nod. "I'm afraid it might not be that easy, though. There are people who play Bingo who have not won for a long time. I think for those people who keep losing, it is hard to see one person win over and over. For them, I think when some-one like Lilly keeps winning it becomes more...how should I say it...magnified."

"Are you speaking about someone in particular?" Alice asked, her head tilted at the end of the question.

"Flo Morgenstern," Bess quickly answered. "Flo has not won in a quite a while. I believe if she were to win, it might ease the suspicions she's been having about Lilly."

"Of course," Alice nodded. "Well, Lilly will only be with us for another month or so. She's being moved to an intensive care unit for treatment."

Alice paused for a moment. She lifted the tissue from her lap and placed it up her sleeve.

"Do you think I am wrong?" she asked, her eyes locking on Bess.

"I think it is good to help a friend," Bess quickly answered. "It is hard to say what makes cheating acceptable, though. Does having a dying friend make it okay to cheat? I don't know. I do think it is nice of you to give her something positive to think about every week."

"Can we keep this our secret?" Alice asked. "I do love helping out on Bingo night. If word got out that I was helping someone to win...well...I may be asked to stop participating with Bingo at Honey Hills."

"Your secret is safe with me," Bess replied. "Just don't forget to let Flo win next time. It will help to alleviate her suspicions."

"I will remember Flo," Alice said with a nod. "Thank you."

The following week, Flo arrived for a Tuesday morning game of bridge with a wide smile on her face. Bess said a polite good morning and watched Flo practically float into her chair. The expression of sheer bliss on Flo's face was not lost on the other ladies at the table. Helen Gruber gave Bess a knowing glance before clearing her throat.

"You look like you swallowed a tickle bug, Flo," Helen observed.

"Yes," Bess said, trying to play along. "Why are you so happy this morning?"

"They had a Bingo night last night," Flo announced. She glanced around the table and let out a small laugh. "I won two times."

"Twice!" Bess shouted, then caught herself and tried to stay calm. "You won two times? Why that's wonderful, Flo. I guess you were due to win."

"My mother used to say that good things come in bunches," Flo said. "Last night I guess my bunches came at the Bingo table."

"Was Lilly Shumocker there?" Helen asked. "I heard her cancer has come back in a bad way."

"Yes, yes," Flo said with a wave of her hand. "She won, too. She didn't win twice like me. In fact, I was the only one to win two times last night. I was so happy I went back to my room and wrote my name in my Bingo journal right beside Lilly's name."

The words caused Flo to stop talking. It was as if, Bess thought, the mere mention of Lilly's name had tripped something in Flo's memory about last week. Bess watched as Flo slowly turned towards her.

"The night you came with me to play Bingo, Bess," Flo began. Her eyebrows went down and her smile melted into a serious expression. "I forgot to ask you if Lilly is actually cheating when she wins at Bingo. You told me you'd find out and you never told me."

"Lilly?" Rose Grumbine finally spoke up. "She would not cheat, Flo. Bess, please tell us that Lilly hasn't been cheating at Bingo"

Bess smiled. Technically, Lilly wasn't aware of what was happening. She was merely doing what most people should do, not questioning when good things happen and enjoying the moment when it did happen.

"No," Bess responded. "Lilly has not been cheating to win at Bingo."

"Oh," Flo replied.

Bess watched as Flo's eyes blinked for a few seconds, as if absorbing the news through her eyeballs before she resumed her very detailed account of her two winning Bingo rounds. As she listened, Bess smiled and couldn't help but think that Flo was a lot like Lilly in how she enjoyed the moment and chose not to question the good things that had come her way. For the rest of the morning, all the ladies at the bridge table got more Bingo tips from Flo than they had in previous mornings. While Bess was happy for Flo, she couldn't help but hope that Flo wouldn't be so fortunate, or that Alice wouldn't be so generous, the next time there was Bingo night at Honey Hills.

A DIRTY HABIT

Of all the nurses employed by the Honey Hills Retirement Home, the one that smiled the least was Nurse Dora Simmons. In the months that she'd lived there, Bess had taken note of every nurse she had encountered at Honey Hills. There were some nurses who came into her room and smiled when they gave her a drink or some crackers. There were other nurses who, on occasion, would enter her room with a smile and ask Bess how she was doing or if she needed anything. Bess even took note of those nurses who passed her in the hallway and greeted her with a kind word and a smile. All in all, most every nurse had some kind of smile to offer the residents of Honey Hills. Dora Simmons was a nurse with a different disposition.

With her wide dark eyes, tan skin, and dark hair that bobbed around her shoulders, Nurse Simmons looked to be a bit younger than Bess's daughter, Samantha. While Nurse Simmons was very polite and very knowledgeable in answering questions, the most challenging thing about her job seemed to be her smile, Bess thought. This challenge was never more apparent to Bess than one afternoon when Nurse Simmons walked into Bess's room, sat down in a chair for the first time, and gave Bess a very serious, direct, unflinching stare.

"Nurse Simmons," Bess finally said after a few uncomfortable seconds of silence. "Is there something wrong?"

"No," Nurse Simmons quickly replied. She drew in a deep breath and let out a sigh as if she were contemplating her next choice of words. "I have something I want to tell you, Bess, but I don't know where to begin. I've been hearing stories from some of the other residents about you. We both know that gossip is something that everyone here enjoys. Lately, I've been hearing some of the residents tell the same odd stories about you. I was wondering how you would respond to these…rumors."

"Rumors?" Bess said, sitting up in her chair. "Rumors about me? Are they rumors of an unflattering nature?"

"Oh no," Nurse Simmons said, her face changing into something close to a smile. "They aren't mean stories, Bess. It's nothing like that at all. In fact, it's just the opposite. What I'm talking about are very positive stories being told about you."

"Then what are these stories?" Bess asked, feeling a need to probe a bit.

"Well, let's see," Nurse Simmons began, rubbing her hands together and looking up in the air as if one would drop into her lap. "I believe one I heard was about you stopping a patient from being smothered to death by a pillow. Another one involves you discovering our therapy dog was stealing items from other residents' rooms. Another story has you being the one responsible for calling the police and having a drug dealer arrested for growing a marijuana plant in our courtyard a few months ago. Are all of these things true?"

"Oh my," Bess said with a wave of her hand. "Do you really think a grandmother like me would be responsible for such things?"

Her comments caused Nurse Simmons to look down at the floor. Bess did not want to get in trouble for her actions. While she knew her actions were beneficial to others, Bess was not about to let Nurse Simmons know about her investigations. By admitting to the validity of the stories, Bess was concerned that she would be told that she had broken some Honey Hills Retirement Home rules in solving the mysteries. If there was one thing Bess did not want to do, it was get on the bad side of Nurse Simmons.

"I was actually hoping the stories *were* true," Nurse Simmons replied. Bess watched as Nurse Simmons grew silent, rubbed her hands together and let out another long sigh. Her eyes appeared to be locked on the floor and, for a moment, it seemed to Bess that Nurse Simmons was lost in her own thoughts.

"Is something wrong?" Bess finally asked. She wanted to reach out and take Nurse Simmons's hand or pat her on the back, but she just didn't feel comfortable offering such affection to the nurse that most residents referred to as "Sergeant Simmons."

"It's nothing," Nurse Simmons said, looking up at Bess.

"Please," Bess continued. "If it was nothing you wouldn't be sitting here staring at the carpeting in my room."

"It's silly," Nurse Simmons replied with a half-smile.

"Then share it with me and we can laugh about it together," Bess continued to press.

"Okay," Nurse Simmons finally said with a shake of her head. She cleared her throat, laughed to herself, and then looked Bess in the eye. "I haven't had a cigarette today."

"A cigarette?" Bess said in a curious tone. She could feel her eyebrows go down at the nature of the words. "If you are here looking for a cigarette I'm afraid I don't smoke. In fact, I believe there's no smoking allowed anywhere in Honey Hills."

"Yes, I know that!" Nurse Simmons snapped. She stood up and folded her arms. "This is my problem. I work during the week and have off on the weekends. During the week when I work I have two breaks in which I can go out to the courtyard to smoke. It's a dirty habit, I know, but it's also a very difficult habit to break. Anyway, when I leave for the weekend, my locker has a full of box of cigarettes in it. When I come back to work on Monday, I check my locker and find that my cigarettes are missing. This has happened for the last two weekends. I usually buy my cigarettes by the box because it's cheaper, but whoever is unlocking my locker and taking them is costing me a great deal of money."

"I see," Bess nodded. Without hesitation, she could hear her instincts begin to kick in. She could actually hear her instincts formulating words and speaking to her mind specifically about the lock that was being opened. Finally, Bess gave voice to her instincts. "You used the word 'unlock.' Does this mean you have a lock on your locker?"

"I bought a lock when this first started to happen," Nurse Simmons answered.

"Does anyone here know the combination to your lock?" Bess asked.

"I just bought a lock that requires a key to open it," Nurse Simmons explained. She pointed to her chest. "I have the only key. I have no idea how someone is opening my locker and taking my cigarettes."

"Are you missing anything else from your locker?" Bess asked.

"No," Nurse Simmons replied.

"And you say this occurs just on the weekends?" Bess asked.

"Yes," Nurse Simmons answered. "I hate to spend my weekend guarding my locker, but that seems to be my only alternative."

"Why don't you take your cigarettes home?" Bess asked. "Bring just a few in when you want to smoke them?"

"I can't take them home. It's just too complicated to talk about," Nurse Simmons said gripping her hands together. "That's just not an option. They have to stay here. I can't keep them at home."

"I see," Bess nodded, sensing a longer explanation lying just beneath the surface. "Well, tomorrow is Friday. Perhaps I could keep an eye out for your cigarettes when Saturday arrives."

"Would you?" Nurse Simmons asked with a slight smile.

"Of course," Bess answered. "I for one would like to know how cigarettes can disappear from behind a locked door."

"Thank you," Nurse Simmons sighed. She stood up and waved Bess along with her to the door. "If you come with me I'll show you where I keep my cigarettes."

Bess did as she was told and began to follow Nurse Simmons out the door of her room. Suddenly, Nurse Simmons stopped in the doorway and turned around to Bess.

"What is it?" Bess asked.

"Are you sure those rumors about you aren't true?" Nurse Simmons asked, with the first broad smile Bess had seen since she came to Honey Hills.

"I'd suppose every rumor has a hint of truth," Bess smiled back, then followed Nurse Simmons into the hallway.

A few minutes later, Bess found herself standing in a small, cluttered room with a sign on the wall that read, "Nurses Locker Room." The more Bess looked around at the cramped quarters, the more she thought it resembled a closet more than a room.

A small row of lockers were located against the far wall. The lockers were about four feet high, gray, with various scratches and dents. A bench was located across from the lockers. Bess watched as Nurse Simmons walked to the second locker from the right, grabbed hold of a lock, and pulled out a small key to open it. Once opened, Nurse Simmons reached into the top shelf of her locker and pulled out a red and white cardboard box. She handed the box to Bess.

"Look underneath it," Nurse Simmons instructed.

Bess turned the red and white box upside down and found that Nurse Simmons had used a black marker to write the words, "Property of Nurse Simmons" on the bottom of the box.

"If you see anyone carrying a box of cigarettes like this one, find out who they are," Nurse Simmons instructed. "Then check the bottom of the box to make sure it's mine. I'm counting on you, Bess. I hope we can get to the bottom of this problem."

"I hope so too," Bess replied, feeling a bit more weight on her shoulders for solving this particular mystery.

THE CIGARETTE THIEF

The next day, Bess chose not to share her conversation with Nurse Simmons to anyone. It was hard to get through Friday without mentioning her latest investigation, but Bess did not want other residents to approach Nurse Simmons about her smoking. In fact, Bess only saw Nurse Simmons once in the hallway during the day. Even for that moment, Bess thought, Nurse Simmons was not able to bring herself to smile at Bess.

"Discretion is the best way," Bess told herself more than once throughout Friday. She found these words especially valuable when surrounded by friends in the dining hall or in the hallways. The words, Bess told herself, acted as an anchor and kept her from foolishly announcing her intent to help Nurse Simmons find her cigarette thief.

When Saturday arrived, Bess was relieved to finally begin her investigation. After thinking about it all day Friday, Bess decided that observation would be her best approach for this particular mystery. Once she finished her breakfast, Bess brought a good book and found a sofa that gave her full view of the door to the nurses' locker room. The only downside about the location where she was sitting was that she was next to a bird cage with a very chatty parrot with sky blue feathers. The bird greeted Bess with a variety of squeaks, chirps and actual words. All the noise made it rather difficult for Bess to concentrate on her reading.

"His name is Phil," one lady stopped to inform Bess.   The woman pointed at the cage and proudly announced, "He's a very smart bird. I believe I was told he knows fifteen words."

"Really?" Bess replied, lowering her book. "Fifteen words. He is truly a very smart bird to know so many words."

In the hours that followed, Bess tried to read her book. In between passages, she managed to count fifteen different words that were uttered by the bird. She also thought she heard a sixteenth word that was too naughty for birds or adults to say. All the while, Bess enjoyed the time to sit, think, and keep one eye on the door to the nurse's room.

Occasionally, she would see one nurse duck in and come out in less than a minute. They were easy to spot, wearing white shoes, white pants and shirts that were very colorful. Every so often Bess would see a woman, dressed in casual clothes, slip into the room only to emerge a few minutes later as a nurse dressed in white shoes, pants, and a nurse's top.

As she remained seated and watched the door, Bess could not help but think about the questions presented to her by this situation. How was someone opening a locker with a pad lock on it? Who would have access to the key to the lock? Also, why was someone only interested in taking her cigarettes rather than stealing something of greater value?

Bess pondered the questions, allowing them to sink in and hoped that perhaps something deep inside of her would speak in reply. Would her instinct have an answer to such questions? She waited for some part of her that would give voice to a clue or a reason for how to pursue this particular investigation.

It was at this point in her thinking that Bess watched a gray-haired woman emerge from the locker room. She had noticed her slip in earlier, and Bess made a mental note that she was clearly the oldest woman to enter the room thus far. When she saw her emerge, Bess noticed she was not dressed like a nurse. In fact, she had on the same blue jeans and purple shirt that she wore when she went into the room. The older woman was also carrying a white plastic bag, which Bess did not notice before. Bess stood up, and decided this woman was worthy of being followed.

Pursuing someone though the winding hallways of the Honey Hills Retirement Home was quite a challenge for Bess. In one respect, she needed to remain a good distance away but she also didn't want to remain too far so as to lose the woman in question. She needed to figure out a way to get a look inside of the woman's bag, but how would she get close enough to do it? How would Bess manage to get this woman to stop?

As she watched the woman walk by a nurses' station, Bess spotted a five dollar bill lying out on the counter. Drawing closer, Bess could see that the nurses' station was unattended, so Bess reached out and scooped up the five dollar bill when she walked by. With the five dollar bill in hand, Bess hurried her pace.

"Excuse me!" Bess called out.

When the woman stopped and turned, Bess quickly raised the five dollar bill in the air and waved it. If there was one thing that would draw people to her, Bess thought, it was the lure of lost money being found.

"I believe you dropped this," Bess said handing the money to the woman.

"Well, thank you," the woman smiled, taking the five dollar bill and examining it.

"Must have dropped out of your pocket," Bess said, glancing down at the bag.

"I didn't realize I had it," the woman laughed.

"Maybe the cashier slipped it into your shopping bag," Bess suggested, pointing down at the bag and getting a good hard look at what was inside. There she spotted what appeared to be the red and white box that Nurse Simmons had shown her just one day earlier. With the woman holding money in one hand, and the bag in the other, Bess took the liberty of reaching into the bag and pulling out the box.

"Hey!" the woman yelled.

"You aren't Nurse Simmons!" Bess stated in a loud voice, pointing at the words printed on the box. "This doesn't belong to you! Why are you stealing this?"

"Who are you?" the woman yelled back.

"I'm someone Nurse Simmons asked to protect her cigarettes," Bess stated with a tone of voice that was equally loud. She held the red and white box up. "I know this doesn't belong to you. Why are you trying to take it."

"Because Nurse Simmons made me a promise," the woman replied. "She's not keeping her promise so...I'm helping her to do it."

"How can stealing something be helpful to anyone?" Bess asked.

THE RIGHT CHOICES

"Yes," the woman replied, her face growing flushed. "I will admit that I am stealing this box, but only because I love my daughter. You see, the person who is breaking her promise is my daughter, Dora Simmons."

Bess looked down at the box in her hands. She turned the box a couple of times, glancing at the name on the box.

"What is your name?" Bess asked.

"Ethel," the woman replied. "Ethel Simmons."

"So you're the one who has been taking your daughter's cigarettes for the last few weekends?" Bess asked.

"Yes," Ethel replied.

"The cigarettes are in her locker and she keeps it locked," Bess explained. "How do you unlock it?"

"I bought her the lock," Ethel stated. "It came with a spare key. I never told her. That's how I've been able to take her precious cigarettes."

"I see," Bess nodded, still holding the box. "Like you, I also have a daughter. Like you, I have times where I do not always agree with her choices."

"Smoking isn't good for her health," Ethel said in an angry tone. "I've told her that more than once. Her father died because of his smoking habits."

"Really?" Bess nodded. "My husband also died from the same thing. His cancer moved very quickly in his lungs. It was because of his smoking. He smoked right up to the end."

"Dora used to smoke a pack of cigarettes a day," Ethel recalled.   She pointed at the box that Bess was holding.   "It looks to me like she's still smoking that much."

"On the contrary," Bess stated.   "The nurses here get two breaks during their shifts.   Your daughter told me she gets two chances to smoke a cigarette during her shift and that is it.   Does she still smoke at home?"

"No," Ethel quickly answered.   "We tossed out all the cigarettes at home.   She knows I'll throw away any cigarettes she brings home.   I guess that's why she keeps them here."

"I see," Bess nodded, now understanding why Nurse Simmons was so insistent about keeping the cigarettes in her locker and not taking them home.

"So why?" Ethel asked, her voice growing softer. "Why won't she listen to me.   I've talked to Dora about her father.   I've told her how much I need her.   Why won't she listen?"

Bess could sense the frustration in Ethel's voice. Here was a mother having difficulties with her daughter, a situation Bess could relate to all too well.

"Yes," Bess nodded, sitting down on a nearby couch.   "I've often thought about how different my daughter's life would be if she had just made the choices that I wanted her to make.   How uncomplicated her life would be if she'd just listened to me over the years."

"Exactly," Ethel said, pointing at Bess and sitting down on the couch beside her.   "Why must I drive in here and steal things from my own daughter's locker?   Why can't she just listen to me and stop this dirty habit?"

Both ladies sat silent for a moment, thinking about their daughters and the challenges they still faced as mothers.   In her mind, Bess could not help but see the image of Samantha checking her watch and talking on her cell phone.

"You know," Bess finally spoke. "The more I thought about it over the years, the more I realized that my daughter may not have made the choices I would, but most of her life I think she's always tried to make the right choice. Trying to make the right choice, to me, seems to be better than always making the wrong choices in life."

"My daughter is still making a wrong choice," Ethel quickly stated, reaching over with her hand and tapping the box that Bess was holding on her lap.

"Is she?" Bess replied. "She's gone from smoking a pack of cigarettes a day to two cigarettes a day. I'd say that's a pretty good choice and a step closer to quitting. My husband never would have been able to live on two cigarettes a day. I think your daughter has made a choice that she thinks is right."

The observation seemed to surprise Ethel Simmons. She grew silent, her eyes moving away from the hall to the cage where Phil the parrot was reciting his vocabulary for anyone who cared to listen. Ethel watched Phil for a moment, then looked back down at the cigarette box and bit her bottom lip.

"If you take this," Bess said, holding up the box. "I suspect she will go out and buy more cigarettes. I suspect that's what she's been doing. If you talk to her, tell her how proud you are of her efforts, she may continue to try to quit."

"Maybe," Ethel replied. She smiled and pointed at Bess. "You must promise me that you will keep an eye on her. Promise me you will be certain to remind her not to smoke more than two cigarettes. Promise me you will help me to encourage her to stop."

"I will do my best," Bess smiled.

"Thank you," Ethel nodded, reaching out and tapping the box once more. She looked at Bess and tilted her head to one side. "Why are you doing this? I don't even know your name."

"My name is Bess Bullock," Bess smiled. "I'm doing this because we are mothers. I believe mothers need to help each other from time to time. Don't you agree?"

"I do," Ethel replied, holding up the five dollar bill that Bess gave her. "Guess I'm going to stop for a cup of coffee on the way home. Isn't it a good feeling to find money? It's just such a nice surprise when good things happen unexpectedly."

"It is indeed," Bess answered.

She watched Ethel stand up and walk away. Bess looked down at the box in her lap. She flipped it over and saw Nurse Simmons' name staring up at her.

"Guess I'd better put you back," Bess said to the box.

She stood and began to walk back up the hallway to the nurses' locker room. As she passed by the nurses' station she heard one nurse asking the other a question.

"Did you see the money I laid here on the counter?" one nurse asked the other.

The second was reading something and merely shook her head in silence.

"I know I put it here a minute ago," the nurse continued. "I was going to get some coffee and a doughnut."

Bess picked up her pace and quickly moved up the hallway. As she walked, she realized that the money she had used to catch up to Ethel Simmons had produced something more satisfying than a cup of coffee or a cream filled doughnut. It had given two mothers a chance to talk and to gain some peace of mind.

On Monday morning, Nurse Simmons approached Bess in the hallway. There was no smile or expression of satisfaction on her face, Bess noted. Nurse Simmons had a look that was not one of someone who appeared to be pleased with the outcome of the cigarette investigation.

"Bess," Nurse Simmons began, "I wanted to thank you."

"Did you talk to your mother?" Bess asked.

"We talked," Nurse Simmons nodded. "I told mom that she needs to keep her nose out of my business. I know she wants me to stop smoking, and I'm gonna try, but she can't just come in here and steal my things."

"I agree," Bess nodded. "It is hard being a mother, though. I want the best for my daughter as your mother wants the best for you.. Your mother and I spoke about that. She knows what I mean."

"I hope," Nurse Simmons said. Her dark eyes flickered over Bess for a few seconds, as if she were measuring her up for a new dress. She stepped closer to Bess. "So all those stories I've heard about you...they're all true?"

Bess merely looked at Nurse Simmons, choosing not to say anything but the smile on her face perhaps answered the question.

"So why do you do it?" Nurse Simmons asked. "Why do you take the time to help solve problems for people?"

"I really don't know," Bess replied. She drew in a breath and pondered the question. "When I first moved here, I was prepared to lead quiet days. I thought I'd play Bingo, do craft classes, join a book club, and just keep busy with fun things. I thought my days would be filled with fun. However, I never imagined how much free time I'd have on my hands."

"Isn't that good?" Nurse Simmons asked. "I mean I just can't wait to have a few days off from this place. I like having free time to read or visit friends."

"I'd suppose a little time off isn't a bad thing," Bess replied. "Sometimes when free time comes in such great abundance, I have a tendency to indulge in bad habits.

Habits that I promised myself I'd break when I moved here."

"You sound like me talking about bad habits," Nurse Simmons said with her first smile of the conversation. "What are you talking about? Smoking? Drinking?"

"No, no," Bess said with a wave of her hand. "When I first moved here, I told my daughter I'd retire and enjoy quiet days here at Honey Hills. I told her I wouldn't indulge in my habits as a detective anymore. They are the kind of habits that seem to keep pulling me into other people's problems. I'm trying to enjoy a quiet retirement, Nurse Simmons. I just need to trust in the good in other people...and not be so suspicious."

Nurse Simmons sat silent for a moment. She looked at Bess and didn't say anything. It was as if Nurse Simmons was still listening to the last few words Bess had just said, even though she was just a foot away from her.

"It seems to me that there are worse habits to have," Nurse Simmons observed. "I don't know how helping people can be considered a bad habit. Perhaps helping other people with their problems isn't the kind of habit you should break. I mean, I'm glad you helped me with my problem. You helped both me and my mother with what you've done. I'm sure the other people you've helped feel the same way. Thank you for helping me this weekend, Bess. Perhaps one day...we will both break our habits."

As Bess watched Nurse Simmons walk away, she thought about what she had said. Was it really such a bad thing to help others? Was it really so terrible to continue to entertain her habits for observation and investigation? Was she really meant to be retired?

GOOD MOTHERS

Saturday was a special one for Bess. It was Nicole's fifth birthday. Samantha and Nicole came to the Honey Hills Retirement Home and picked up Bess early in the morning. When they arrived at Samantha's house, the rest of the morning was spent cleaning, arranging balloons, wrapping gifts and preparing Nicole's favorite meal; hotdogs and macaroni and cheese. It was a hectic morning, and Bess was pleased to find that she could keep up with the pace and the work that had to be done.

Around noon time, the young guests and their parents began to arrive in the backyard to Samantha's house. Bess found a lawn chair under the shade of a maple tree where she decided to sit and watch the festivities unfold. Every so often, a soft steady breeze played across the leaves and splashed across her face, providing some relief from the heat of the day. Looking out from her seat, Bess had a perfect view of all the guests and the various activities taking place.

Pink and purple balloons were strung around the yard, and twirled against a bright blue sky. Across the way, she could see a table of presents wrapped in brightly colored shades of yellow, pink and orange shades. The smell of hotdogs lingered in the air, causing Bess's stomach to rumble more than once. She could also see the parents standing and talking while they ate from tiny paper plates and drank from paper cups. Around the yard there were Nicole and her friends, running and laughing while they weaved in and around the parents.

Fluttering around the grown-ups and the children was Samantha. Always with a smile on her face. Always moving smoothly with plates or cups in both hands. On occasion, Samantha would actually stop and have a conversation with one of the parents in attendance. Bess noticed how Samantha would nod, smile and acknowledge every word spoken to her. It occurred to Bess that Samantha had grown up to become a very good listener...when she didn't have her cell phone. Bess also could see how much other people enjoyed knowing Samantha was listening to what they would say. The world, Bess often thought, needed fewer talkers and more listeners.

A little while later, Samantha called everyone to a picnic table at the center of the yard. Bess spotted the birthday cake on the table and made her way over to help. When she reached the picnic table, she found ten little girls piled onto the two benches on either side of the table. Bess smiled at their faces, each bright red and glistened with sweat. At the center of the pile was Nicole, leaning on the table with both elbows, lingering closely to a chocolate birthday cake. Samantha lit the candles on the cake, nestled down on the bench beside Nicole, and led everyone around the table in singing "Happy Birthday."

As she sang, Bess watched the faces of the two most important girls in her life. Nicole's face was filled with excitement and happiness. Her eyes were as wide as Bess had ever seen them. They danced back and forth from the large cake in front of her to the many faces that surrounded her. Her smile was so broad, Bess thought, her cheeks looked like two small balloons that were about to burst.

Next to Nicole was Samantha, who was smiling just as brightly and just as broadly as her daughter. Yet, while Nicole's eyes were dancing between the cake and the people around her, Samantha's eyes were locked on one thing and one thing only. Bess noticed how Samantha's eyes were so focused on Nicole that they didn't even blink. Nicole was clearly the source of all of Samantha's happiness. Bess thought that if someone brought in a million dollars, it wouldn't cause Samantha to look away from her daughter. If Bess could take this moment and place it in a bottle, she would keep it for both mother and daughter to enjoy over and over again. It was clearly such a special moment, Bess could feel her heart tingle.

When the singing was done, Nicole closed her eyes with great anticipation then blew out her candles. Everyone clapped, causing Nicole's head to whip around and raise her hands in the air like some performer who had just done a magic trick. Bess turned to Samantha, who was now preparing to cut the cake.

"Excuse me," Bess said, stepping around some of the girls who were gathered around the picnic table. Bess grabbed a stack of paper plates and made her way over to Samantha. She handed Samantha the first plate to lay a piece of cake on. For the next few minutes they stood shoulder to shoulder, Samantha placing pieces of cake on plates and Bess passing them out to the guests. Together they worked until everyone in the yard was eating. When they finished, Bess and Samantha stood at the table and watched the festivities around them.

As she watched the party, it seemed to Bess that all of the differences between herself and Samantha were a million miles away. Her savings, the lawyer's papers, the tension over their last conversation at the Flower Fest were now just a dim memory in comparison to this bright happy day.

"You're a good mother," Bess said, gently rubbing Samantha's back with her hand.

"Thanks, Mom," Samantha said. She turned to Bess and for the first time in weeks actually smiled at her. Bess watched as Samantha reached down, sliced off a piece of cake and put it on a plate. She handed the dish to Bess and said, "So are you."

Bess accepted the cake, and the words, with a smile. Samantha cut herself a slice and took a few bites of the cake. Together they stood in the yard looking around and enjoying the day. Both were aware that it was a special day that could only have been made by two good mothers.

A NEW BEGINNING

Bess held onto the good feelings from the birthday party for a few days. It was most enjoyable to watch Nicole laugh and play with her friends. What Bess liked most was the opportunity to be around the boundless energy of young children. Listening to their voices, watching their activity, it all combined to give Bess a feeling she hadn't had since she moved into the Honey Hills Retirement Home. While she enjoyed the silent confines of Honey Hills, sometimes silence needed to be replaced with laughter, loud voices, and occasional squeals of enthusiasm.

Bess thought about this on a morning when there was a more enjoyable task to be done. It was a Tuesday morning, the favorite day of the week for Bess. She made her way down to the Game Room where she was surprised to find only one person seated at the table, rather than the three she had expected. She walked in to find Flo Morgenstern busily shuffling cards and laying them out on the table. When Flo looked up to see Bess standing in the doorway, she scooped up the cards in her hand and smiled.

"Thought I had the wrong day," Flo said, looking a bit relieved that her mind had not let her down. "Where are Rose and Helen?"

"I don't know," Bess replied. She sat down at the table next to Flo. "Perhaps they got confused and forgot today was Tuesday."

"Maybe," Flo nodded. "I don't know about you, but it gets me mad when I forget a date or a name I should know. Sometimes, when I get confused about things, it gets me a little worried, too. I mean, let's face it Bess, we're not youngsters anymore."

"I know what you mean," Bess smiled. "Sometimes I feel as though I need to be at my best when my daughter comes around. You know, she wants me to sign one of those papers so she can take care of me if I can't take care of myself. I'm not ready for that to happen. I like taking care of myself and I like that I don't have to depend on other people to do it. So yes, those moments when I am a bit forgetful or confused do upset me as well."

In the moment of silence that followed her words, Bess looked out the window at the bright sunshine that was striking a field of tall green corn stalks. She could hear Flo shuffling cards behind her and turned around to watch. Suddenly, Rose Grumbine appeared in the doorway. Bess watched as Rose quietly walked in the Game Room and stopped by the table. She did not pull out a chair to sit down, which Bess thought rather odd.

"Looks like we're all a little late this morning," Bess smiled.

Rose remained silent and showed little expression.

"Is something wrong?" Flo asked, putting the cards down.

"Last night," Rose began. She paused, her eyes blinking quickly and her face looking flushed. "Helen had a heart attack and died."

"What?" Bess asked, smiling at the oddity of the news.

Rose quietly sat down and cleared her throat. Bess could feel herself leaning towards Rose, hanging on any more words she could add to this already strange news.

"It happened late last night," Rose began. "She called the nurses to her room because of chest pains. The nurses checked her and called an ambulance. By the time the ambulance arrived she was…gone."

"Oh, dear," Flo sighed while shaking her head. "Oh, poor Helen."

"Perhaps I should talk to the nurses," Bess offered. "Maybe there was something they could have done. Or maybe I could find out how long it took the ambulance to arrive. I wonder if the nurses could have done more for Helen?"

"Stop it, Bess," Rose said, her voice growing louder.

"I was just curious about what happened," Bess stated.

"Not everything is a mystery," Rose said with a sharp tone. "Helen had a heart attack. She died. That's it. That's how life works. There are no clues to be found or secrets to uncover. It's life, Bess, that's all."

Bess grew silent at Rose's words. Indeed, she had been thinking of this as some kind of mystery. Rose was right, Bess thought. There was no mystery about what happened to Helen. She was gone and there was nothing Bess could do to bring her back.

"Will there be a funeral service?" Flo asked.

"Helen has family in Kansas," Rose stated. "I don't know if they'll fly her back there. I think she told me once she wanted to be cremated. Right now, I think everyone is just in shock."

"That's understandable," Bess said, slowly rubbing her hands on the table top. "Well, if you hear anymore please stop by my room and tell me."

"Me too," Flo added.

"I'll keep both of you updated," Rose said before quietly leaving the room.

The news of Helen Gruber's death came as a shock to Bess. She spent the better part of the next couple days thinking about Helen. While she knew Helen on a social level, and enjoyed chatting with her about gardening and cards, what Bess found most unnerving wasn't her death but the idea of dying.

When she moved to the Honey Hills Retirement Home, Bess tended to think of it as a vacation. There were new people to meet, new things to do, and new places to see. Once she settled in, Bess allowed herself to become distracted by the various little mysteries of Honey Hills and its residents. However, what Helen's death had done was reawaken a thought that Bess had unintentionally pushed back into the darkest corner of her mind.

For the last nine months, Bess never gave much thought to the fact that she had come to Honey Hills to die. Somewhere between dancing with Chet, playing bridge with the ladies, and the occasional Bingo night with Flo, Bess had forgotten all about the notion that she had moved here and would not leave until her life was over. She sat in her room one morning thinking about this revelation when she heard a knock on her door.

"Come in," Bess said.

She watched the door open and saw Alma Crisp appear. It was the first time she'd seen Alma since the incident with her granddaughter. She wore a bright orange top, white pants, and matching orange shoes. Her hair was perfectly arranged and she had bright red lipstick on. Now that she was better, Bess thought, Alma was back to being the best dressed resident at Honey Hills.

"Morning, Bess," Alma said with a smile that caused more wrinkles to appear around her cheeks. "Just wanted to stop by to say "thank-you" for everything you did for me and Hannah."

"Oh," Bess said with a wave of her hand. "Anyone would have done what I did, Alma. It's just nice to see you back the way you ought to be."

"Thank you," Alma said, lowering her head. She took a step closer. "I also wanted to say I was sorry to hear about Helen. I know she spoke of you often. She and I sat at the same table for our meals, you know. She always came to lunch and dinner with a good story that would make everyone laugh."

"Did you know she was from Kansas?" Bess asked.

"I didn't know that," Alma replied, shaking her head. "We'd just have fun talks over our meals. You know, stories and things that would make us laugh."

"Helen was fun to talk to," Bess mumbled.

Alma walked over to where Bess was sitting and sat down on the chair beside her.

"How are you doing with all this?" Alma asked.

"Oh, I'm fine," Bess explained. "I mean, I liked Helen and she was very funny, like you said. What's bothering me is the fact that she died here. We're all going to die here, aren't we?"

"There are worse places to die," Alma pointed out. "My uncle died on a battlefield during a war in Europe. Could you imagine all the loud sounds, the foul smells, the soldiers yelling and you have to lay there and die? Honey Hills may not be ideal but, like I said, there could be worse places to die."

Bess nodded at the comment. She thought of her father and took a deep breath.

"You know my father was a policeman," Bess began. "When I was little I remember how much my mother used to worry about my father getting shot or dying when he would go to work. They would talk about it sometimes when they thought me and my sister were upstairs sleeping. I remember my father would always tell my mother not to worry about how things might be but to worry about how things are."

"Live for today and not tomorrow," Alma nodded. She said the words again and smiled. "That sounds like good advice to me."

"Yes...I guess it does," Bess said. For the first time today, she could feel a smile on her face. She took a deep breath and could feel the stress and worry leave her body. It was as though her father were sitting in the room offering Bess the same advice he gave her mother. Advice that helped Bess calm down. Suddenly, Bess sat up in her chair and pointed to Alma.

"Do you play bridge, Alma?" Bess asked.

"I know how," Alma replied. "It's been a long time since I played, though. Why?"

"Some friends and I like to play bridge on Tuesdays," Bess explained. "Since Helen has died, we can't very well continue to play without a fourth. Would you consider joining our group since Helen is gone?"

"That sounds splendid," Alma replied with another wrinkly smile. "Who's in the group with you?"

"Rose Grumbine and Flo Morgenstern," Bess replied.

"I know Rose," Alma nodded. "She's very nice. I've seen Flo at some of the Bingo nights, too. She's a very good Bingo player."

"That's what Flo tells me," Bess said with a smile.

"It sounds like a nice group," Alma said, standing up. "I would be honored to join you. Tuesday morning you say?"

"That's right," Bess stated. "We meet in the Game Room around nine o'clock."

"Then I shall see you next Tuesday morning," Alma grinned before walking out the door.

As she watched the door to her room close, Bess thought about what had transpired. During one conversation, her mind had resurrected words from her father. Words that had helped to comfort and calm her feelings about the events of the morning. Indeed, it was too much to look at life's large canvas and try to take in everything that was there. Bess could very easily spend her days at Honey Hills worrying about when and how her death would occur. She could also spend the same amount of time worrying about when or how her daughter or granddaughter would one day die for that matter.

Rather than letting such worries get her down, Bess decided it would make more sense to heed her father's advice and worry about today. Right now, that meant thinking about the invitation she had just extended to Alma Crisp. Bess wondered how Rose and Flo would react to the news and decided to keep it a secret until next Tuesday morning.

A NEW PLAYER

For the next week, Bess kept marking off the days on her calendar. Every morning she would use a bright red marker and make a large red X through a particular day. She couldn't wait for Tuesday to arrive so she could introduce Rose and Flo to the newest member of their Bridge Club. Helping to start the Bridge Club was one of the best things Bess had done since moving to Honey Hills. With Helen's death, Bess was hopeful that they could continue the meetings. She was nervous and hopeful that Alma would slip right in with Flo and Rose.

The day that Tuesday finally arrived, Bess made a point of going to Alma's room and knocking on her door to walk her down to the Game Room. When Bess opened the door, there was Alma in an aqua blue sport shirt and white slacks with matching white shoes. Judging by her appearance, Bess guessed, it seemed Alma was also treating this as a special occasion.

"Ready to play?" Bess asked.

"Oh, yes," Alma quickly answered, stepping out of the room. "I've been looking forward to this ever since you invited me."

Together both ladies made their way down the hallway. Together they turned a corner, then another before finally arriving at the Game Room. Bess led Alma into the room where they found Flo and Rose already seated at the table. Bess noted how both Flo and Rose's faces looked up in surprise, only to see their mouths melt into easy smiles.

"Alma!" Rose grinned. "Good to see you. We were just talking about Ruth Moore. Did you know she's turning one hundred tomorrow?"

"Yes," Alma smiled, glancing over at Bess. "I heard that from one of the nurses."

"Can you imagine being a hundred?" Flo chimed in. "I heard they're going to be serving cake and ice cream at her party. I'm going to have to go just for the cake. I love cake."

"Me too," Alma replied with a smile.

"So what brings you here this morning?" Rose asked.

"I thought Alma could join us for bridge," Bess quickly explained. "If that's okay with both of you."

"Fine with me," Rose nodded, glancing across the table at Alma. "I think Alma would be a wonderful addition to our little club. We all know her and like her. What do you think, Flo?"

"That would be fine with me too," Flo replied. "I mean, I'll miss Helen but I'd want to continue our Tuesday morning card games. Besides, we can't play bridge with three players."

Bess and Alma quickly sat down at the table and watched as Rose held a deck of cards in her hand. She reached down with one hand and grabbed hold of something under the table. With a grunt, Rose managed to pull up what appeared to be a large golden canister.

"Is that…" Bess began, pointing at the container and unable to finish her question.

"It is," Rose quickly answered.

"That's Helen?" Flo asked, sliding her chair back from the table.

"Yes," Rose replied. "The family flew in from Kansas yesterday. They agreed to let Helen come to one more morning of bridge before she leaves. It seems Helen spoke quite fondly of us. The family thought it would be nice if we could all say something about her before she goes back to Kansas."

The room grew silent at the end of the request. Bess couldn't tell if the other people in the room were as comfortable with this as Rose appeared, or if they were a bit uncomfortable at having someone's cremated remains in the room. While she knew it was Helen, Bess could at least admit to herself that her silence was due to the oddity of the moment and not because of her contemplation over what to say.

"I'll start," Rose finally announced, standing up and clearing her throat. She turned to the golden canister and stood up. "Helen, you were the one who invited me to join this group. I will always be grateful to you for that. I hope you find peace where you are and friends that you can continue to enjoy playing cards with every Tuesday morning."

When she sat back down, her eyes turned to Flo Morgenstern. Flo slowly got to her feet and turned to face the gold container.

"Helen," Flo began, pointing uneasily at the container as if it were a person. "I hope they still play bridge wherever you are and I hope you continue to win your fair share."

"You're always worried about winning," Rose mumbled under her breath.

"I believe that's why God made games," Flo said with a shrug. "He made games for them to be won."

"Please say something," Rose said, rolling her eyes to Bess.

"Okay," Bess said, quickly standing up. "Well, uh, Helen, I want to thank you for helping me feel like I belong here. When I first came, you would always stop playing bridge long enough to listen to me and my problems. I always appreciated that. I also want to thank you for helping me to dig up that chicken with the bright red pants."

"I knew that was you two," Flo said, pointing at Bess.

"Anyway, Helen," Bess continued, glaring across the table at Flo. "Thank you for being such a good friend. I hope I can be that kind of friend to Alma Crisp."

"Oh, Bess," Alma smiled. "If I could just add, Helen, I hope you find a place where you can spend some time with people as special as Bess, Rose, and Flo. We will miss you."

With those last words, Bess sat back down and all the ladies smiled and looked at one another. Rose quietly shuffled the cards and passed them out to Flo, Bess and Alma. When the final card was dealt, Rose looked around the table, took in a deep breath and said,

"Ladies, let's play cards."

As the game began, Bess couldn't help but think that this was just how life worked. One week they were saying goodbye to a friend, and the next week they were beginning a new game of bridge. It was, Bess thought, the clearest example of how there was never an end to life, merely a pause for mourning before it continued on.

A CENTURY BIRTHDAY

The next morning Bess woke up to find a flyer that had been slipped under her door. She picked up the paper and focused on the bright pink letters on the sheet. As she read, she realized she was holding an invitation to a birthday party. It seemed that a huge party was being held in the Honey Hills Social Hall for Ruth Moore, who had just turned one hundred years old. The invitation also stated that music and snacks would be provided for all to attend. While Bess fully expected to live to be one hundred like her parents, the incident involving Helen Gruber had created some doubts in her mind. Going to the party, Bess reasoned, would be the right kind of medicine to cure those doubts.

When she arrived at the Social Hall, Bess saw a large bouquet of balloons strung up from the ceiling. All different colors floated above her, as if someone had grabbed hold of a rainbow and pulled it inside for this very special day. On a long table next to the door, Bess saw a variety of pictures from Ruth Moore's life. There were some pictures of her as a young girl with curly blond hair. There were other pictures of her as a young mother, holding a baby with curly blond hair. What Bess found most interesting were the pictures of Ruth when she was much older. There were pictures of Ruth when her hair had turned white and she was now wearing glasses. She was clearly much older, Bess thought, yet there Ruth was standing on the Great Wall of China. Another picture showed Ruth standing next to a sign indicating she had journeyed to Niagara Falls. Yet another picture was of Ruth standing in a city street with the Eiffel Tower looming tall in the background. Suddenly, Bess had great admiration for Ruth Moore. Here was a woman who had continued to travel well into her golden years, which is exactly what Bess had planned to do. Her eyes then turned to a woman sitting in a wheelchair, with white hair and a matching white sweater. It was Ruth Moore.

Bess watched as Ruth chatted with a couple that was visiting. While she spoke, Ruth held a bowl of ice cream in one hand and scooped it out with a small spoon in the other. Bess noticed how Ruth would nod at some of the comments, and on occasion would stop eating to say a few words here and there. It seemed to Bess that even at one hundred, Ruth was still a very good listener on a day when those in attendance should have been doing less talking and more listening.

Bess carefully waited for a couple to finish talking to Ruth. After a few minutes, she heard Ruth tell the couple to take care. The words made Bess smile to herself. Hearing someone of one hundred years telling a clearly younger couple to take care of themselves made her laugh. If anything, Bess reasoned, the sentiments should have been made by the other party and not by Ruth. When the couple left, Bess spied a good moment to slip into a conversation.

"Good morning," Bess said, standing in front of Ruth. "I don't think we've met. My name is Bess Bullock. I live here at the Honey Hills Retirement Home and I just came to wish you a happy birthday. I just think it is wonderful to have someone here who is one hundred years old."

"Thank you, dear," Ruth replied. She carefully placed the bowl of ice cream on her lap and folded her hands. Bess noted the curve in her fingers and guessed it was a mild case of arthritis. "It's been a goal for me to live to be one hundred, you know. I'm just so happy that I was able to do it."

"I was admiring your pictures," Bess said, gesturing back to the table. "You really took a lot of trips when you were older."

"Oh yes," Ruth nodded. "When I first came here I told the Honey Hills staff I wanted to travel to three countries. They were kind enough to get in touch with a local travel agency and found some groups that were close to my age. Traveling to China, Canada, and France were just wonderful experiences."

Bess sat down on a chair next to Ruth. She leaned close and took the empty bowl of ice cream off her lap.

"You know," Bess began. "Both of my parents lived to be one hundred. I plan on doing the exact same thing. I would love to travel and do things like that. What's it like to be one hundred years old?"

"Oh, I would recommend it," Ruth laughed with a soft chuckle. "There are so many things you will experience. I can remember all the presidents, the historical events, the famous people who have come and gone. It really is something to live this long."

"So what's your secret?" Bess finally asked, leaning in a bit.

"Keep your mind active," Ruth quickly answered. "I read a book a week. I do crossword puzzles. I even sit by my window and count cars by the hour sometimes. I've thought of all these ways to keep my mind engaged. Some of my friends weren't able to do that and they had all kinds of problems. So that's my advice to you. If you want to live to be a hundred, Bess, you need to keep your mind alert and active."

"Thank you," Bess said, standing up and allowing another couple to start a conversation with Ruth.

As she walked around the room, Bess looked at the familiar faces packing the room. She looked at the faces and felt herself smile. She saw Alma Crisp, perfectly dressed and laughing with her friends. There was Charlotte Lapp walking with her daughter who was holding baby Jonah. There was Chet Wooden, his blue eyes focusing on Bess from across the room. He smiled at her and Bess began to rub her hands together, as if willing them from holding Chet's hand. She even saw Bart the therapy dog walking on a leash with a nurse.

When she took in the sights around her, Bess realized that as long as she stayed at the Honey Hills Retirement Home, she was confident that there would be many more mysteries to occupy her mind and keep her engaged. Right now, she felt as though reaching one hundred years old was a very real goal.

THE FLIGHT

The following morning Bess sat on her bed, fully dressed, looking out the window at the darkness that filled her window frame. Though she would normally be asleep at such an early hour, this morning was anything but normal. Today was her birthday. After months of anticipating turning eighty, Bess had finally achieved her goal. It was an age that her older sister had never lived to see, which gave Bess a strange feeling knowing she was now older than her big sister.

While she sat on her bed, Bess was nervously anticipating her birthday present. For weeks, she had been planning her airplane flight as a gift to herself. There was something about the age of eighty that simply required a special celebration. Seeing the sunrise in the valley from an airplane was something she had always wanted to experience. This morning, her anticipation would finally become a reality.

"What will it be like?" Bess asked herself. Her mind began to race. Would the clouds be white, pink, or gold? Would she see any birds? Would she fly over the mountains? Would she see any deer or bear running along the mountain paths? The images of what was to come fired her imagination and caused her to swing her legs from her bed like a school girl.

A gentle knock on the door brought the images in her mind to stop. When she slid off the bed, she heard the soft knock again. Bess opened the door to find Chet

Wooden standing in a pair of dress pants and a button downed blue dress shirt which matched the blue in his eyes.

"I feel a bit dressed up for this early in the morning," Chet smiled. He reached out and gave her hand a playful squeeze. "Happy Birthday, Bess."

"Thank you," Bess answered, stepping out into the hallway and closing the door. "I'm really glad you're coming with me, Chet. I simply couldn't do this flight alone."

"This will be fun," Chet smiled, leading her out of her room and down the empty hall.

Together they made their way outside. Chet directed her to a long silver car that he still owned. Bess watched as Chet quickly walked ahead of her, opened her door and helped her inside. She smiled at the gesture and the expression on his face.

Together they drove for just a few minutes in the darkness. Bess noted how all the homes they drove by were dark. One or two lampposts were left on, but she couldn't find one window in a home that was illuminated. It seemed to Bess that the rest of the world was asleep. They drove for just a few minutes from the Honey Hills Retirement Home to Tucker Airport.

Surrounded by farm fields, Tucker Airport was a small, privately owned airport. A handful of planes were stored and maintained in the two small hangars located on the airport's grounds. In fact, the airport was so small Bess was told that it was actually run and maintained by a gentleman named Hank Tucker and his three sons. The size of the airport mattered little to Bess. What did matter was the opportunity to fly into the morning sky.

When they arrived at the airport, the sky was a mix of dark blue and black. The air had a slight nip to it. Bess looked east to a bright orange crest that was burning behind two dark sloping mountain ridges.

"Mrs. Bullock," a young man asked, bouncing up to her with some spring in his steps. "Are you Bess Bullock?"

"I am," Bess replied. She turned and gestured to Chet. "I brought a friend along for the flight. Is that okay?"

"Same price for one or two," the young man answered. He brushed his dark hair to one side and smiled. "My name is Wally Tucker. I'll be your pilot this morning. You got any questions before we go up?"

"Not really," Bess answered.

"Over here's our plane," Wally said, leading Bess and Chet to a small twin engine plane. The plane was white with two blue stripes along the sides.

"Got earplugs here if you need them," Wally said, holding out his hand to reveal small round plugs.

"Not for me," Bess said. "My hearing is already a little off. Ear plugs won't make much of a difference."

"I'm fine, too," Chet said with a wave of his hand.

"Okay," Wally smiled. He looked up to the deep dark blue sky. "If we time this right we should be able to see a beautiful sunrise. Why don't you two hop in and we'll get right up there to see it."

Bess nodded and followed Wally to the plane. She grabbed hold of the door frame and Wally helped her in. Bess sat down in a seat closest to her and fastened a seat belt. She looked around and saw how tight the space was for this trip. Chet followed her in and sat in the seat next to her. Wally closed the door, locked it, then ran around to the other side. He opened the door to that side of the plane and climbed inside.

"He looks awfully young, doesn't he," Bess whispered to Chet.

"Everyone looks very young to us," Chet laughed.

"Here we go!" Wally called out, then turned the engine on. It was loud. Bess leaned over and yelled something to Chet, but he still couldn't hear her.

The hum of the engine seemed to shake the cockpit. She looked out the window and held her breath as the grass began to slowly pass by her window. She watched as the grass moved faster and faster. The vibrations from the plane's wheels filled her seat, then quite suddenly grew calm.

She held her breath as the plane slowly ascended from the landing strip and into the air. Her stomach felt like a hundred butterflies had just been released. She reached out and grabbed Chet's hand as the plane smoothly glided up and over the farm fields that surrounded the small airport. She looked at Chet, his eyes were wide and his smile ran up both sides of his face. The expression of joy on his face helped Bess to relax a little.

In the distance, she could see the sun appear in one corner of the valley. It was a shade of red she'd never seen before. The sun was round, but sagged a bit in the middle, taking away from its perfectly circular shape she was used to seeing most mornings.

Below, she could see an evenly shaped square field of amber wheat that the plane was now over. She looked beyond the wheat field and could see a patchwork of green and golden fields and farms. With its uneven slopes and gentle crests, the land reminded Bess of a quilt that was covering a hastily made bed. Green, brown and amber fields seemed to unfurl in all directions throughout the valley. She looked more closely at one field, and could see an Amish farmer driving two horses and a wagon.

Bess turned her eyes to the rim of the valley and she could see that the mountains were now starting to gather colors for autumn. She tapped the pilot on the shoulder and pointed towards a line of mountains. She felt the plane swerve and her wish was granted. When they flew closer to the ridge of the valley, Bess found each of the mountains to be a unique blend of bright red, orange and yellow colored trees at their peaks. The pilot took the plane lower, and Bess felt her heart race. She squeezed Chet's hand a little harder when she saw the trees come closer to the plane. Soon her vision was filled with a dizzying array of trees filled with red, gold and orange colors. The autumnal colors raced by her eyes at a dizzying pace.

She looked over at Chet who was gazing out his window. He turned to her, the colors of the trees spilling around his head and shoulders. Bess looked down at her hand for a moment, then pulled Chet's hand closer to her. She looked up at his face, feeling herself growing lost in his eyes.

Her vision was filled with the red, orange and gold colors flowing around him, then she centered her eyes on his. She leaned in closer. All she could see were the bright blue color of his eyes. Soon she felt his warm lips meet her lips, and her heart raced while she felt his body lean into her. Her eyes were filled with either blue sky or Chet's blue eyes, she was no longer able to distinguish between them. The plane glided up. Her feet tingled. Her heart flew.

OLD HABITS

That evening Bess sat in her room reflecting on the day. She thought back to the morning and that most memorable airplane ride. She thought about the kiss that she shared with Chet and could feel her face grow warm from the memory. She smiled when she recalled the residents in the Dining Hall who sang Happy Birthday to her and presented her with a birthday cake after supper.

"If only every day could be a birthday," Bess sighed to herself.

As she sat in her chair, lost in her memories of the day, a knock on the door interrupted her train of thought.

"Come in," Bess called out.

She watched the door open and a small woman appeared. She took a few steps into the room. She was a short woman, with thick glasses that made her eyes appear to be twice their normal size. Her gray hair had a blue tint to it. She appeared to be nervously picking at her fingers when she entered.

"My name is Millie Cord," the woman announced. "I'm looking for Bess Bullock. Are you her?"

"Yes," Bess smiled in an attempt to help her visitor relax.

"Are you the one who located Chet Wooden's wallet after it was stolen from his room?" Millie asked with a nervous smile.

"I am," Bess answered without hesitation.

"I also heard you helped the police find a drug dealer, is that also true?" Millie asked, her hands shaking as she tugged at her fingers.

"It is true," Bess replied again without hesitation.

Unlike her discussion with Nurse Simmons a few days earlier, when Bess declined to take credit for her investigations, she found herself not trying to be as coy with Millie. Perhaps she was trying to be reassuring, Bess told herself, or perhaps she was simply tired of hiding her accomplishments.

"I have a problem," Millie announced, continuing to pick at her fingers. "I understand you are someone who helps people with their problems. Is that true?"

Bess paused for a moment. Was this going to be how she was to spend her time at the Honey Hills Retirement Home? Was she indeed going to use her skills for observation and investigation to solve problems for others? She looked at a Millie, who was clearly nervous and still picking at some skin on her fingers. Bess waved Millie over to a chair across from where she was seated. Millie quickly sat down and folded her hands on her lap.

"Someone is borrowing one of my dresses," Millie quickly stated.

"Excuse me?" Bess replied.

"Someone is coming into my room when I'm not there and taking a red dress from my closet," Millie stated. She nervously patted her bluish gray hair with her hand and cleared her throat. "It's happened two times, now. Both times, the dress was returned washed, ironed, and laid out on my bed. I must admit, it's actually been returned in better condition than I would keep it. Still, I don't like having someone go through my closet and wear my clothes."

"I think that would make me just as uncomfortable," Bess nodded.

"Can you help me?" Millie asked.

Bess sat back in her seat.   When she first moved into Honey Hills she fully expected to fill her days with idle activities like cards, Bingo and puzzles. She thought retirement was going to allow her to spend her days as she wanted. However, she now knew that was not who she was.

Bess had uncanny instincts to observe people and investigate little mysteries.   She couldn't turn those instincts off and she didn't want to change who she was. Her instincts gave her a purpose in her life and now they would give her some meaning in her retirement, too. After all, Bess told herself, if she was going to live to be one hundred she couldn't just sit around watching TV and eating chocolates. Retirement wasn't going to include idle time for Bess. It was going to include investigating the little mysteries in life and helping others in the process. That was who she was, Bess thought, and she wasn't going to change because of her age or because she was retired. She turned her eyes to Millie, who was nervously picking her fingers and patiently waiting for Bess to answer her question.

"Yes, Millie," Bess finally said with a direct unwavering tone in her voice. "I can help you with your problem."

THE END

Allen B. Boyer is the author of two Young Adult novels and one nonfiction book about the West Point Academy and its famous graduates. His books have been sold around the country. This is his first cozy mystery novel.

Mr. Boyer lives near Hershey, Pennsylvania, with his wife, Suzanne, and their three children. He likes to take his children and their dog to visit residents at a nearby retirement home.